Frank Bolles

Land of the Lingering Snow

Frank Bolles

Land of the Lingering Snow

ISBN/EAN: 9783337252991

Printed in Europe, USA, Canada, Australia, Japan

Cover: Foto ©Andreas Hilbeck / pixelio.de

More available books at **www.hansebooks.com**

LAND OF THE LINGERING SNOW

*CHRONICLES OF A STROLLER IN
NEW ENGLAND
FROM JANUARY TO JUNE*

BY

FRANK BOLLES

BOSTON AND NEW YORK
HOUGHTON, MIFFLIN AND COMPANY
The Riverside Press, Cambridge
1891

The Riverside Press, Cambridge, Mass., U. S. A.
Electrotyped and Printed by H. O. Houghton & Co.

CONTENTS.

	PAGE
FOOTPRINTS IN THE SNOW	1
NATURE IN ARMOR	6
A TEMPEST	12
THE SEA IN A SNOWSTORM	18
TWO VIEWS THROUGH WINTER SUNSHINE	25
WAVERLEY OAKS AND BUSSEY HEMLOCKS	31
THE FIRST BLUEBIRDS	38
THE MINUTE-MAN IN A SNOWDRIFT	44
THE COMING OF THE BIRDS	51
THE EQUINOCTIAL ON THE DUNES	59
THE RENAISSANCE	73
THE VESPER SONG OF THE WOODCOCK	78
A TRIP TO HIGHLAND LIGHT	83
THE CURRENT OF MUSKETAQUID	98
A BIT OF COLOR	110
THE CONQUEST OF PEGAN HILL	115
WOOD DUCKS AND BLOODROOT	122
A VOYAGE TO HEARD'S ISLAND	130
A FOREST ANTHEM	149
THE BITTERN'S LOVE SONG	159
WARBLER SUNDAY	165
ROCK MEADOW AT NIGHT	176
THE SECRETS OF THE MEADOW	181
WACHUSETT	190
IN THE WREN ORCHARD	198
CHOCORUA	208

LAND OF THE LINGERING SNOW.

FOOTPRINTS IN THE SNOW.

SUNDAY, the eleventh day of the new year, was what most people would call a good day to stay in the house. The face of New England winter was set. No smiling sky relieved its grimness, no soft breeze promised a season of relenting. The notes of the college bell were muffled and the great quadrangle was deep with snow, as I left Old Cambridge behind me and sought the hills of Arlington three miles or more to the north. Slowly climbing the heights, after my car ride, I looked back at the world I had left. The sky was a mass of dull gray clouds, with a copper-colored spot where the sun was hiding. Boston and Cambridge lay under a pall of smoke and dun-colored vapor. The broken ridges from Belmont to the Middlesex Fells were buried deep in snow, the soft whiteness of which was interrupted by patches of dark pines, dotted with stiff cedars, or shaded by the delicate etching of birches and elms. The air was in that condition which favors the carriage of distant sounds. I heard the rumble of trains on the Fitchburg, Massachusetts Central and Albany railways on the one hand and of those on the Northern roads on the other. Now and then the tooting whistle of a train sounded like the hooting of a mammoth owl.

Entering the woods, I found written upon the snow the records of those who had travelled there before me. A boy with his sled had been across to a pond in the hollow. A dog had followed him, running first to one side, then to the other. Further on I struck another track. The prints were smaller than the dog's, round, and in a single line, spaced quite evenly, like those of a fox. Somebody's cat had been hunting on her own account. In an open space, bunches of goldenrod and asters had been pulled to pieces, and all around their stalks the footprints of small birds, perhaps goldfinches or redpolls, were thick. Not far away the snow on an open hillside was pencilled by the rising stems of barberry bushes. From the pine woods to these bushes numerous tiny paths led. The most dainty feet had printed their story there. The journeys seemed to have been made in darkness, for the paths made queer curves, loops, false starts into the open pasture and quick re-

turns to the woods. The barberry bushes had
been found, however, and were thoroughly en-
snared in the tracks. The mice which formed
them had made holes in the snow near the stems
of the bushes, and these holes led through long
tunnels down to the ground and possibly into it.
Among the pitch pines, old orchards, and chestnut trees squirrel tracks were countless. Most
of them were those of the red squirrel, but in
deeper woods I found records of gray squirrels
as well. Along frozen brooks, where alders,
willows, privet, and rosebushes were thick, the
small brown rabbits had been feeding and pay-
ing moonlight visits to each other. In an orchard I found a place where a crow had alighted
and marched about with long strides. Most interesting of all were the hurried tracks of a
flock of birds which had been feeding on barberries, juniper and privet berries. They had
been disturbed by a dog and had skurried
through the thicket, their sharp toes printing
innumerable "crow's feet" in the snow. What
were they? I pushed on to see, and soon started
a flock of fifteen quail from a dark grove of
pines. Later I found one cuddled up in a hollow in the snow under a juniper, eating the berries over her head. I nearly stepped upon the
bush before she flew.

Descending into a ravine filled with ruddy

willows, privet, and rose bushes gay with their red hips, I heard a note which made me halt and listen. Yes, a robin. The sides of the ravine were clothed with savins, the ridges were crowned by tall pines. Rose hips and sumac seeds, barberries, privet and juniper berries furnished food, and the sun is always warm — when it shines. A soft rain began to fall, and it loosed the tongues of the birds. Chickadees called from tree to hedge. Golden-crested kinglets lisped to each other in the cedars. A dozen crows circled over the high pines, cawing discontentedly, and the robin's note sounded from three or four quarters at once. I gained the top of the ridge and looked across a pasture. In a branching oak were several birds. As I drew near, others flew in from neighboring savins and bunches of barberry bushes. They were robins. In all, thirty-six flew into the oak and then went off in a noisy flock as I reached the tree. Their plumage was much lighter than in summer. The rain fell faster and I left the pasture, homeward bound. The last I saw of the pasture hillside it was sprinkled with robins running back and forth on the snow, picking up privet berries. They were as jolly as in cherry time.

While recrossing pasture and field, swamp and thicket, I noticed countless black specks upon the snow. They moved. They were

alive. Wherever a footprint, a sharp edge of
drift, or a stone wall broke the monotony of the
snow surface, these black specks accumulated,
and heaped themselves against the barrier. For
miles every inch of snow had from one to a
dozen of these specks upon it. What were
they? Snowfleas or springtails (*achoreutes nivi-
cola*), one of the mysteries of winter, one of the
extravagances of animal life. Fortunately they
prefer the cold face of the snow to a life of para-
sitic persecution.

As I caught a homeward-bound electric car,
I looked back at the ridges of Arlington with
gratitude and admiration. They made a landscape of ermine, a soft blending of light and
dark. The falling rain, snowbound farms, savin-
dotted hillsides, bluish belts of woodland, delicate tracery of elm branches ; all mingled to
form a background for reverie, a gentle good-by
to a day of rest.

NATURE IN ARMOR.

NATURE does not always drop her cloak of ermine when she buckles on her armor. She often covers her soft snow garments with icy mail and meets the dawn with every hillside a shield and every branch of oak a sword. She was thus girded and armed on Sunday, January 18, 1891, as I sought the Arlington hills at the hour when the air of Suffolk and Middlesex was throbbing with the music of church bells. A gentle east wind — for even Massachusetts east winds can be gentle when they try — carried in slanting lines against the hills and trees a steady fall of cold rain. It had been falling so for over twelve hours, till level snow, fences, walls, weeds by the wayside, shrubs, orchards, elms in the meadows, savins on the hillsides, and belts of woods on the ridge-crests were all sheathed in clear ice, which measured, on an average, a quarter of an inch in thickness.

As I mounted through the open fields toward the heights, I wondered what the birds were doing in the cold rain, with every twig ice-coated, and every berry shut up in thick crystal. Where were the crows, the chickadees, and above all, the adventurous robins? "Here I am," a robin seemed to say from the roadside, and at the same instant I saw a bird fly from a dense tangle of briers, bushes, cedars and tall maples, to the highest branch of a tree, shake himself thoroughly, and then give the familiar robin signal of alarm and inquiry. He was answered by a second bird, and presently three of them flew over my head and down the hill towards a grove of pines. I had a clear view of them through my opera-glass.

A few steps further on I came to a white birch-tree, bent by the ice till its head rested in a snowbank on the opposite side of the road from its but. It formed an ice-screen thirty feet long and nine feet high, directly across the road. The tree measured nearly three feet in circumference at its base. Near by a grove of white birches had become a shapeless tangle of ice-wires and cables. The eye could not separate any one tree from the mass, and the tops of all were resting upon the snow. The road was lined with bleached asters and goldenrod. Not only were their stems ice-hung, but their pale, flower-like involucres were embedded in nodding balls of ice, half an inch in diameter. So delicate were these mock flowers and so erect and perfect their form within the crystal, that it seemed certain they must have been first embraced by a freezing mist as gentle and caressing as a ray of sunshine. The same ice-kiss had rested upon the bunches of red barberries, the dark berries of the privet, and the sticky, red, cone-shaped masses of the sumac fruit. Even the dead, russet leaves hanging from the oaks had a sheet of ice clinging to them which, when slipped off, showed their form and veinings.

Entering the pine woods where I had previously seen quail, I found the trees in trouble. The great pines were loaded down with ice, and many a branch had broken and fallen under its weight. The surface of the snow was strewn with twigs and branches of every size. A strange roar of falling ice and twigs filled the woods, now and then emphasized by the crash of some greater fall. I found the tracks of one quail and of a rabbit, made doubtless Saturday evening while the snow was still soft; but otherwise the face of the snow told no tales. It was smooth and shining, as though no dainty feet of mice and squirrels had ever pressed upon it. There were squirrels at work, however. Under one pitch-pine I found a pint of cone chips freshly strewn. Half a mile distant I surprised a red squirrel busy in an old chestnut-tree which had succumbed to its awful burden of ice and fallen mangled in the snow. He fled from me and bounded up the trunk of an oak, but he reckoned without the ice, and when part way up lost his grip and fell back upon the crust below, a very much mortified squirrel.

In dense growths of pitch-pines and savins I came across six flocks of chickadees, in all perhaps twenty of the merry little birds. They seemed to keep dry, and by working on the under and westerly sides of the branches found food not covered by ice. In one of the flocks were two little brown creepers who were unable to make spirals or zigzags round the tree-trunks, as is their frequent practice, but who seemed happy in hitching straight up the trunks of the pines and the oaks. The chickadees, creepers and crows, as well as the robins, were very talkative. The only other bird seen was a small hawk, which sailed silently over the snow in a secluded pasture.

About two o'clock I gained the crest of a high ridge from which I could see many miles of snow-covered country. The sky was a cold grayish white; the pines and cedars looked almost black. Against the sky the ice-covered, leafless trees were a darker gray than the clouds, but against the evergreens or in masses by themselves they were ashes-of-roses color and wonderfully soft in tone. Looking across a sloping pasture at a swamp filled with elms and willows,

they seemed to be a mass of dark stems with
their tops shrouded in pale smoke through which
the faintest possible fire-glow permeated.   I
suppose the color came from the reddish bark
of the twigs.   Just then the sun found a rift
in the rushing clouds, and for a single minute
poured his glory upon the crystal world below.
Every tint changed.   Every atom of ice responded, flashing to the touch of light, but the
east wind hurried forward fresh mists from the
ocean and the sunlight vanished.   Below me
hundreds of small trees trailed their tops upon
the snow.   It seemed as though some muezzin
of the ice-world had called them to their prayers.
Farther away were acres of scattered pitch-pines,
every bunch of whose needles was a drooping
pompon of heavy ice.   As I looked at them
through the thickly falling sleet they seemed to
march in ranks across the fields of snow, their
heads bent from the wintry storm, despair in
their attitude.   " The retreat from Moscow," I
said, and hoped that the day of judgment against
the weak among the trees would not be followed
by a night of tempestuous wrath against the
whole ice-bound forest.

The wind, gentle as it seemed, was too strong
for some trees.   Once I heard a report like a
cannon, and turned to see an old willow forty
feet high plunge into the snow.   At another

time a long branch of an elm at which I was looking slowly bent lower and lower, and then broke midway with a crack and swung toward the ground. I raised a prostrate cedar bush, whose height was about seven feet, and found that its load of ice seemed to weigh thirty pounds. If this were so, what must the burden of the great trees have been? Tons, perhaps. Yet the oaks did not seem to bend an inch. Their stiff heads were raised straight toward the sky, and their immovable arms bristled with icicles.

About an hour before sunset I pointed my course downward, sighting for the tower of Memorial Hall rising black against the distant sky. Much ice had fallen from the trees since the forenoon, and there was a ceaseless roar of falling fragments as I passed through the strips of woodland. The temperature had risen enough to loosen the ice armor, and everything from asters to elm-tops was casting it off.

A TEMPEST.

On the afternoon of Saturday, January 24, while roaming over the hills between Arlington and Medford, I made up my mind not to spend the next day in the woods. Nature seemed to have become prosaic, almost dull. I saw one crow, — no other tenant of the woods. The snow had been washed away and the ice which remained was stained. The air was heavy with the breath of long-forgotten cabbage-leaves. Farmers were at work in their plowed lands, stirring up other odors equally obnoxious. Even the fields were unpleasant to walk over on account of their alternate patches of ice and pasty mud. But Sunday morning before sunrise the wind shifted to the northeast and changed a drizzling rain into a furious snowstorm, and by noon, when I reached the first hill-top above Arlington, the storm was at its height. The air was in a fury. Laden with great masses of flakes it bore them in horizontal lines over fields and pastures, hurling them against every obstacle, and whitening even the window panes of houses facing eastward. The blast was as unintermittent in its pressure as natural forces can be ; yet it seemed to excite vibration and rhythm in all it touched. The tops of the pines fell and rose, the branches moved forward and back, the roar of the wind pulsated and the soft surface of the snow was not even, but broken into tiny waves. In the pine woods the wind was less violent, but the passing snow seemed like vibrating white lines rather than flakes. As I stood in the pines and looked northeast, every tree was black against a distance of on-coming white rage. As I looked southwest every tree was white, finely outlined in black, against a retreating mass of colorless motion. If I looked southeast the trees were black and white, and if northwest they were white and black, and whichever way I looked the air was surging on, laden with the bewildered and bewildering snow.

Pushing on I entered a deep and rocky gorge. Possibly Verestchagin's brush could indicate the absolute whiteness overlaid upon the less absolute white of that mysteriously beautiful spot. Certainly nothing else could. Every rock, bush, trunk, limb, branchlet, twig and leaf-bud was covered with the clinging snow. Beyond was an oak wood. The inelastic ice of last Sunday failed to bend these stubborn trees, but the wet, sticky snow had overcome them. Dozens of slender young oaks, thirty feet in height, were bent to the ground. This gave a hint of what the condition of the pitch-pines and cedars would be, in spots sheltered from the wind, and I hurried on to see them. The walking was heavy. Early in the afternoon, when the storm abated, just nine inches of snow had fallen on a level. Passing through the woods, where I had seen quail two weeks ago, but where now no sign of them was to be found, I came out into the old pasture, thickly overgrown with savin, pitch-pine and barberries. Here and there something which resembled a tree remained, but the greater part of the growth had been suppressed. There were rounded masses which looked like sheep in the snow, and there were arched stems from which depended balls and branches of snow resembling boxing-gloves, cauliflowers, toy rabbits and lambs and other unpoetical objects. In most cases the top of the pine or savin could not be distinguished from its base.

At the foot of the hill was a cedar swamp. Entering, I could readily imagine myself in the Luray Caverns. A floor of pure white supported an endless series of white columns, beyond which were botryoidal masses of white rising to a roof of white. Mingled with the more regular forms were snarls and tangles of snow serpents, and shafts and pinnacles as varied in form as the stalagmites of the limestone caves. Later I was in one of these enchanting places when the sun came out and the zenith was left free from clouds. The effects were so beautiful and striking that, although words give but a hint of them, they are ineffaceable in memory. Through the swamp runs a small stream. As the day was comparatively warm no ice encumbered the clear water. At one point it spread out over a broad bed of mud, from which rose a thick growth of grass, watercress and ranunculus. All three plants were vivid green and offered a strange contrast to the arabesque of snow which framed the brook.

Wild as was the storm and stimulating as were its direct buffeting and indirect effect of form and color, the day was as remarkable on another account as it was for the tempest. I saw eighty-five birds, representing nine species.

Several times I heard crows, flying through the driving snow, calling to each other in its confusion. In the pines at the summit of the first high hill were two little brown creepers flying from trunk to trunk and exploring busily the bark on the sheltered side of the trees. When they left a tree the storm whirled them away like dry leaves, but they promptly headed toward the wind and sped back under the lee of some sheltering tree to its but, the point where their explorations always begin. They kept track of each other by frequent attenuated squeaks. Chickadees were everywhere, and very noisy. They worked quite as much on snow-covered twigs as on the sheltered side of branches. In the cedar swamp they popped in and out of snow caverns among the branches, often tipping over great piles of snow and dodging them with a jolly "chick-a-dee-dee-dee." In this swamp a single tree-sparrow appeared among the branches of a big cedar and looked with evident amazement upon my snow-covered form. Here, too, I saw and heard the first robins of the day flying and signalling among the tops of some of the larger cedars, and near by in a bunch of pines, just above the swamp, three golden-crested kinglets made merry in the sunlight which succeeded the storm. A solitary goldfinch undulated over me in an open pasture, singing the first note or two of his summer song, and a nuthatch passed close by me on my homeward walk.

But the great display of birds came in the middle of the afternoon, at the time that the clouds were breaking and the wind was working out of the east. I was crossing a high sloping pasture with a cedar swamp at its base and a fringe of large cedars round its edge, when, striking a patch of concealed ice, my feet flew from under me, and I found myself on my back in the snow. Looking into the sky, I saw a flock of at least twenty robins flying overhead. They came from the swamp and stopped in the fringe of cedars to frolic and feed. Suddenly a flock of smaller birds joined them, and by the aid of my glass I discovered that they were cedar-birds. For twenty minutes or more this company of fully fifty birds romped in the savin tops, as they do in cherry-trees in summer, the screams of the robins being incessant. Many of the robins came near enough for me to scrutinize their plumage closely. I saw none but male birds among them. The two flocks vanished as suddenly as they came, and I could find no trace of either, although I searched and waited for them more than an hour. These birds were seen on precisely the same spot as the large flock of robins observed January 11.

Although I did not leave the woods and pastures until sunset with its exquisite tints had come, I saw no footprints of any kind in the snow. I wished that I could linger until evening and follow the soft tread of rabbits and mice, the moon meanwhile pouring her light into the enchantment of those groves of snow-encumbered trees.

THE SEA IN A SNOWSTORM.

FEBRUARY came in under the guise of May.
The sky of Sunday, the first, was wonderfully
blue; its air mild, often more than mild; its
clouds were like the pictures in my old physical
geography. I could almost see the mystic words
cirrus, *cumulus*, *stratus*, written in the heavens.
Tempted by the mock spring I extended my
walk beyond its usual limits, infringed on Lexington, and from the heights of Waverley surveyed miles of glistening hillsides to the north
and west, and crowded cities to the south and
east. Every hollow was a pool, and every glacial furrow in the hills a brook. The cabbages
were reasserting their rights to the farmlands
and the air appurtenant thereto.

The birds revelled in the warm sunshine, flying for the love of flying, and calling loudly to
each other for the sake of calling. The crows
spoke loudest and the chickadees most often. On
a sunny bank a large flock of goldfinches were
feeding among the weeds and grasses. I counted
fifty of them, and several flew away before the
census was finished. They were singing enough

of their sweet song to suggest the summer.
Once during the day I heard the "phœbe note"
of the chickadee, and twice I had the satisfaction
of hearing crows " gobble." They do not often
make this sound. It suggests somewhat the
gobbling of a turkey-cock. So warm, thawing,
and genial was this day that one had to be pes-
simistic to realize that it was only a mocking
grin on the mask of winter and not a smile on
the lips of spring.

But Sunday, February 8, showed winter in
his true colors again. The day was, as regards
snow-laden trees and drifted roads, a duplicate
of the last Sunday in January. Instead of enjoying the snow pictures in the woods and pastures of Arlington, I traversed Crab Alley,
Bread and Milk Streets, and that meandering
marvel of old Boston, Batterymarch Street, and
gained the harbor front at Rowe's Wharf.
Some of these snow-covered haunts of trade
were as free from footprints as the savin
swamps of Arlington. In Crab Alley I came
to tracks in the snow which made me wonder
whether some of the quail from the Parker
House toast had not escaped alive. Dainty
little steps crossed and recrossed the narrow
lane, and formed a dense network of converging
paths at the back door of a small chop-house.
As I approached, two tame doves flew noisily

from behind the barrel which graced the door-step, and several English sparrows swung from a telephone wire overhead.

I looked up into the iron caps of the electric light lamps to see whether the sparrows had built in them. They had. In Boston and sev-eral adjoining cities the major part of these iron witch-caps contain sparrows' nests. Even the lamps which are suspended over the streets and drawn in daily by the linemen are not dis-dained by the birds.

From the deck of the Janus-natured ferry-boat, which was pausing for the time between trips to the Revere Beach cars, I looked out upon a chilly sky and sea. The waters were restless, the wind fierce and cold, the snow-flakes stinging. At anchor lay a large steamer, black and thin. The odd gearing at her stern showed that she was an ocean cable steamer. Beyond her was a four-masted schooner. I wondered what her sailors called her fourth mast. Suddenly my wandering eyes were fixed in astonishment upon a jaunty form floating on the water within less than fifty feet of the ferry-boat. It had emerged from the cold and tossing waters with a bounce, shaken itself, and begun a bobbing career in the daylight and snow-flakes. Pop! Down went its head, up went its tail and feet and it was gone again. During

fifteen minutes it bobbed up six times in the
same spot, staying afloat each time from fifteen
to thirty seconds, and below about two minutes.
It was black above, snowy white below, and
formed in the likeness of a duck. It was a
whistler, a duck common in the harbor and
along our coast in winter. While diving, it was
probably breakfasting upon small shell-fish
found on the bottom.

On the way across to East Boston I saw
seven or eight more whistlers and over fifty
herring-gulls, many of them in the dark plumage peculiar to the immature birds. Twenty
minutes later I stood on the narrow strip of
sand left between the poplar walk in front of
the Point of Pines Hotel and the angry ocean.
The wind was northeast, and blowing a gale.
The tide had turned half an hour before, but it
was still unusually high. Behind me the Saugus marshes were wholly submerged. A few
haystacks alone broke the monotony of gray
water, foam and scudding snow. To the north
ought to have been seen distant Lynn, but the
eye was met only by stinging snowflakes and
cold wind. My train, before it had gone an
eighth of a mile, had been swallowed up in steam
and hurrying masses of snow. Where was Nahant? There was not a trace of it. The hungry waves broke ten ranks deep upon the flat

sands across which they roared; but beyond
them was no land, — only the fury of gray and
white hanging above a hissing, greenish gray
and white below. The sand was brown, not a
warm brown, but a cold, shining, grayish brown
with no kindness in it.

There was nothing in the whole world which
my eye could reach to suggest warmth or happiness. True, there were the empty buildings
with padlocked doors among the snow-covered
trees, but they were more desolate and soul-chill-
ing than anything in nature. I walked among
them until wearied by the mockery of their
signs and broken paraphernalia. Hideous ki-
osks, whose blue and yellow paint was partly
covered by the white pity of the storm, told in
glaring letters of " Ice Water," " Red Hot Pop
Corn," " Sunshades and Fans," and " Clam
Chowder." The wind shrieked through their
cracks and pelted wet snow against their windows. In the amphitheatre where spectacular
plays are given on summer evenings the tide
dabbled with the rusty wheels of a sheet-iron
car marked " Apache." Beyond it, canvas
mountains and cañons were swaying and creaking in the storm, their ragged edges humming
in the wind. A sign offered " Seats for 50
cents, children 25." The seats were softly
cushioned by six inches of snow, but the idle

summer crowd had been blown away by the
winter's breath. Only a flock of a dozen crows
lent life to the arena.

A train emerged from the storm. I could see
its dark outlines; its torn column of steam;
the swift motion of its many wheels, — then it
was gone, engulfed in the dizzy vibration of the
snow, its voice unheard amid the greater voices
of the sky and sea. The tide was going down
as I started towards home on the hard shining
sand of Crescent Beach. I think at least two
hundred herring-gulls passed by me, flying
slowly against the gale and keeping over the
water, but parallel to the beach and about a
hundred yards from it. They were silent.
Their strong wings beat against the storm.
Now and then one plunged into the foam of a
breaking wave, or glided for a second along the
trough of the sea. They did not seem like
true birds, beings of the same race as humming-
birds, sweet-voiced thrushes, or keen-witted
chickadees. They were rather creations of the
salt waves and ocean tempests; cold-blooded,
scaly things, incapable of those loves and fears,
songs and quaint nesting ways of the birds of
field and forest. Near Oak Island a flock of
four snow buntings, which had been feeding
among the bunches of seaweed, rose at my approach and flew toward and past me up the

beach. They are among the most beautiful of
our winter visitors, their white and brown plumage being a sight always welcome to the eyes of
those who love the birds. At intervals flocks of
English sparrows rose from the seaweed and
shunned me. There seems to be no form of
vegetable food-supply upon which our native
birds depend, that this ravenous, non-migratory
pest does not devour.

From Point of Pines to Crescent Beach station the thunder of the breakers and the rush of
the wind and snow were ceaseless. The storm
hurried me along in its strong embrace and drove
its chill through me. The tide had left the
marshes, and the snow had claimed them. As
the waves retreated from the beach the snow
stuck to the gleaming pebbles, the snaky bits of
kelp and the purple shells. Where two hours
before, at high tide, the waves had dashed foam
fifty feet into the air, now the breakwaters and
the heaps of shingle and seaweed were covered
with white from the drippings of the great roof
of sky.

The whistlers were still in the harbor at three
o'clock. but most of the gulls had gone. Snow
clung to decks, masts, yards, furled sails and
rigging. It whitened the water-front of the
city, purified the docks, and made even Crab
Alley seem picturesque as I ploughed through it
homeward bound.

TWO VIEWS THROUGH WINTER SUN-SHINE.

SATURDAY and Sunday, the middle days of February, were filled to the brim with sparkling winter sunshine. The heavens were swept clean of clouds by a rush of cold dry air from the birthplace of the Great Glacier. The ground was like granite, and was well covered with the snow that crunches under foot like pulverized quartz.

I spent Saturday afternoon on the highest part of the Belmont-Arlington ridge, and the world, seen from those wind-swept heights, seemed made of cleaner, brighter stuff than when touched on the flats below. There are clear days in summer, but they are not so absolutely clear as the clearest days in winter. I never saw a more perfectly transparent air than that which raced across New England on that Saturday. The vision was not checked by distance or by vapor; only by the curve of Mother Earth's cheek.

Looking eastward from the heights, the eye passed over the Fell country of Medford and

Stoneham and the marshes of the Saugus to the
irregular line of Massachusetts Bay.   Long
Beach, running out from Lynn to Nahant, was
dazzlingly white against the pure blue of the sea.
Little Nahant, Egg Rock, Nahant and Winthrop
Head, all snow-covered, stood out in bold relief
against the even-tinted water.   Between them
several schooners appeared now and then working up the coast, the sunlight striking full
against their sails.   High intervening land cut
off a view of the wooded and rocky Beverly
shore; but the Danvers Asylum could be
plainly seen, like a great feudal castle, crowning
one of the highest ridges.

Southward a nest of cities rested on the fork
of the Charles and the Mystic.   The chilled
breath of half a million people hung over them
and their crowded homes, but it did not obscure
the picture of the harbor with its forts, islands,
and moving sails, nor the more distant panorama of the Neponset Valley and Hull, Hing-
ham, and the Scituate shore.   This view of
Boston and its densely populated neighbors has
a strange fascination about it.   There is little
beauty in its blending of roofs, chimneys, telegraph poles, church spires, flashing window-
panes and bits of white steam or darker smoke,
yet in spite of its distance and silence it has the
mystery of life about it.   From a mountain-top

the eye may roam over granite peaks, serried ranks of spruce forest, undulating groves of pines and birches, green intervales and snug farmhouses, finding in them a restful charm, a song of sweet New England calm. In this mass of distant houses, factories, grain elevators, stores, wharves, churches, marked here and there by historic outlines like Bunker Hill Monument, the golden dome of the State House, Memorial Hall and Mount Auburn Tower, there is something which stirs and stimulates rather than soothes, something which recalls the toil, sorrow, self-sacrifice and eternal restlessness of society, and the ever-present duty of the individual toward it. The mountain view lulls one's conscience ; the sight of this nest of cities arouses it to action.

Westward the view from the heights was monotonous. Low ridges succeeded each other for many miles, holding in their hollows towns, snow-covered farming lands, broken bits of oak or pine forest, and patches of ice on pond or meandering river. But northward the eye found much to rest upon. Along the limits of Middlesex could be seen the valley of the Merrimac. Then came the border towns of New Hampshire, and beyond them the peaks and rounded summits which are the pride of Jaffrey, Dublin. Peterborough, Temple, and Lyndeborough.

From Wachusett on the left to the Uncanoonucs on the right the horizon was roughened by the mountains of the Monadnock group, snow-crusted and flashing in the sunshine. They recalled boyhood days and adventures. A race from a bull on Monadnock, a moonlight climb on Lyndeborough, a thunder-storm on Pinnacle, a July picnic on Joe English hill.

On the way home I saw a flock of about twenty cedar-birds in the same pasture where I saw them on January 25. They were cold and listless, allowing me to approach them closely enough to see the scarlet wax on their wing-feathers. Two of them were eating barberries which they picked one by one while clinging head-downwards on the bending stems. The robins, I learned from a fellow-observer, had been seen not only that day, but every day for a month, on their favorite feeding-ground. The flock varies in size, he said, from twenty to fifty. As I hurried along over the snow in a very windy field a mouse scampered away from one bunch of grasses to another and plunged into his hole. His doorway was well protected by a large bunch of dried grass.

Sunday I took an early train for Readville, crossed the pretty triple-arch bridge over the Neponset, and climbed to the snowy crest of Blue Hill. Although the hill is nearly three hundred feet higher than Arlington Heights, its view seemed to me less attractive. It is three miles farther from the cities; fifteen miles farther from the New Hampshire line, and in the centre of a country less picturesque in formation than that of the Middlesex Fells. Moreover, a northwest wind, which is the one most likely to accompany clear winter weather, carries the smoke of Boston in such a direction as to injure the Blue Hill view, while it improves that from Arlington.

As I looked down upon the Neponset meadows, Ponkapog Pond and Great Pond, I saw moving black specks which reminded me of the amusing little snow-fleas. They were skaters, enjoying the ideal weather for their graceful exercise. Passing Governor's Island and heading for Broad Sound was a four-masted schooner under full sail. Not a bird was to be seen on the hill. The top is covered with scrub-oak, which is replaced on the slopes by small nut-trees, oak saplings, a few pines, birches and maples. There seemed to be no food for any kind of winter bird. In the estates below, near the triple-arch bridge, I saw crows, chickadees, two tree - sparrows and a downy woodpecker.

As I came back to and through the city by an afternoon train I wondered which was less

wholesome for the eye of man, the dingy
monotony of dirty white houses which one
used to see in suburban streets, or the nause-
ating combinations of yellows, greens, cheap
reds and discouraged blues which are now the
fashion.

WAVERLEY OAKS AND BUSSEY HEM-
LOCKS.

A FEW rods beyond the railway station in
Waverley the tracks of the Fitchburg and Massachusetts Central roads cross a meadow through
which Beaver Brook flows on its way to the
Charles. In this meadow the towns of Belmont,
Watertown and Waltham find a common corner, and here stand the Waverley oaks. Some
of these ancient trees grow on the level land
through which the brook has cut its channel,
but most of them rise from the narrow glacial
ridges which project into or border the meadow.
There are few places near Boston which welcome
spring earlier than this moist and sunny corner.
Here early spring birds are found, and many of
the choicest flowers flourish. Saturday, February 21, was a misty, moisty day with gray skies,
wet snow and rain-laden air. Beaver Brook
meadow was as wet as a meadow can be without
changing its name, and the brook itself was
more than knee-deep.

The meadow, that afternoon, yielded to me
the first flower of spring. It is true I had seen

a golden crocus bud before leaving the city, but
it was under the shelter of a well-warmed, south-
facing house, and had been covered with a
straw blanket all winter. This flower of the
swamp had taken care of itself on the edge of a
cold spring filled with bright green watercress.
It had no warm wall to shelter it, no blanket
save the black mud. It was as large as a tulip,
and its spots and stripes of purple and greenish
yellow made it quite conspicuous in its meadow
bed. Pulling open the fleshy lips of its highly
scented spathe, its yellow pollen was scattered
in all directions. The name of this odoriferous
flower of early spring is *symplocarpus fœtidus.*
Passing through the ancient oaks I heard birds
singing in a stubble field beyond. The oaks are
the finest trees I have ever seen outside of the
primeval forests of the North. One of them —
not the largest or oldest — measured twenty feet
around its trunk at a height of three feet from
the turf. There are in all nearly thirty of these
magnificent trees, whose age, if John Evelyn is
a good authority for the age of oaks, is probably to be reckoned by centuries. The glacial
kame from which these trees spring, old as it is,
bears on its face the record of change and of
the woes of nature; but the oaks, having out-
lived generations of other trees, seem like moun-
tain-crests, stable and enduring. The birds in

the stubble field proved to be tree-sparrows. They were feeding on the seeds of weeds found on patches of moist earth left bare by the wasting snow. Each bird was saying something in a joyous recitative which he maintained continuously, regardless of the rippling mirth of his companions. I crept close to them and watched them through the embrasures of an old stone wall. Their chestnut caps, white wing-bars and long slender tails make them easy birds to recognize. As I rose they flew, nearly thirty strong, and vanished in the mist.

Recrossing Beaver Brook I kept along the Belmont ridge for a mile or more, seeing crows, chickadees, a flock of six cedar-birds, a brown creeper, several kinglets and two grouse, seven species all told.

As sunset drew near the mist became denser. The few springtails which I saw along the stone walls seemed sluggish. While watching them I noticed a tunnel under the snow, made, I suppose, by a field mouse (*arvicola pennsylvanicus*), and running from the wall to a pile of brush in the pasture. It twisted and wound in and out in strange figures. Here and there its maker seemed to have poked his head through the snow to get his bearings. From the length of these tunnels I inferred that their little engineer works either very fast or very long in making them. The snow fell Friday, the tunnels were made before Saturday afternoon, yet one of them was fully three hundred feet long.

At the sunset hour a strange glow permeated the mist, but it soon vanished. I left the hills and crossed the Belmont meadows. The twilight was weird. The mud of the Concord turnpike seemed unnaturally yellow; the pollard willows assumed horrid shapes; head-lights on distant engines made menacing gleams on the wet rails; the great excavations in clay beds near the brickyards were filled with black shadows from which rose vapors; brooks once clear, now polluted by slaughter-houses, gave out foul clouds of mist, and as electric lamps along the road suddenly grew into glowing yellow balls in the fog, they showed, rising above them, crucifixes of this nineteenth century on which are stretched the electric wires whose messages of good or evil keep the nerves of society forever uneasy.

Sunday was a cheerful contrast to Saturday night. With a young friend who was heart-full of love for birds, flowers, the quiet of the woods and the music of the brooks, I tramped from Bussey Woods westward through the quiet lanes, snow-covered pastures and secluded swamps which fill the sparsely settled region in this corner of Brookline and West Roxbury. It is a

charming bit of country crowded with hills, deep
valleys, groves of many kinds of trees, roaring
brooks, fern-hung ledges of pudding-stone, and
sunny orchards. Birds were numerous. We
began with a golden-winged woodpecker in the
great trees of the Arboretum; then a robin appeared and snapped his tail at us from the top
of an elm. The voice of a blue jay came from
the evergreens, and chickadees were everywhere.
From the first bare hill we gained a broad view
of Boston, the harbor and the country from Blue
Hill to Arlington Heights. A fresh west wind
and a bright blue sky made everything seem
full of readiness for spring and a new period of
blossoming growth. Passing Allandale Spring
and gaining a ridge beyond, we heard the mewing of a large hawk, and presently saw a pair
of fine red-shouldered hawks quartering over a
meadow, probably in search of mice. They rose
and perched for a moment in the top of a tall
dead tree. In Walnut Hills Cemetery we found
quail tracks under barberry bushes, and presently flushed a bird. We also saw a kinglet
in the swamp. Red squirrels, mice, rabbits, and
another quadruped evidently very abundant in
the region, had made multitudes of tracks in the
soft wet snow. Just what this other quadruped
was I cannot surely say, but if it was what I suspect it to have been, I should prefer not to travel

much by night in its company. A chipmunk, finding the mouth of his hole free from snow, had come out from it into the driveway and made a few scampering circles where the snow was shallowest.

As we neared the edge of Newton, we saw a downy woodpecker with his red cap on. In the swamp beyond were grouse tracks, and foot-prints of a man and dog. Both the latter had been running, and I fancied the dog had started a rabbit which the man had hurried to head off at a point where a wood-road rounded the corner of the hill. Soon after crossing the Newton line we turned toward the southeast and walked rapidly back to the top of Bellevue Hill. Wa-chusett and Monadnock greeted us from the far horizon, and a marvelous blending of bay, city, park, suburban settlement, and untouched na-ture surrounded us on every side. Fortunate Boston, to be girdled by such diversified and picturesque country! The view from this hill is readily gained by walking from Highland Sta-tion, and it seemed to me more charming than that from Blue Hill.

The last pleasure of the day was in exploring the hemlock woods at the Arnold Arboretum. Thanks to an arrangement with Harvard Uni-versity, the people of Boston have the use of this beautiful estate for all time. While its systematic collections are as yet young and incomplete, its natural beauties are many. Just north of Bussey Street an abrupt rocky hill, crowned with tall and singularly straight hemlocks, rises above the surrounding fields and rolling pastures. From its deeply shaded top looking down its precipitous ledges upon the roaring waters of the Bussey brook, I seemed to feel myself removed from the neighborhood of a great city to one of those wild White Mountain ravines where trout are hidden in the torrents, where the harsh scream of the pileated woodpecker breaks the silence of the forest, and where the hoof-print of the deer is oftener found than the footstep of a man.

THE FIRST BLUEBIRDS.

SOME of the wildest, roughest, and most heavily timbered country within sight of Boston lies in the western end of Winchester and along the northern edge of Arlington. I reached it on the afternoon of the last day of winter, by walking along the western shore of Mystic Pond until near the Winchester line, then bearing to the left until I gained the high wooded ledges which command Winchester village from the west. It was a blustering day: the air was filled alternately with golden sunlight and flurries of large snowflakes. Dry snow covered the ground. Along the stone walls it had drifted heavily, reaching in many places a depth of two feet. Walking in the ploughed fields was uncertain, the furrows being filled with snow and the ridges blown free from it. The brooks were noisy, but their music was muffled by decks of thin ice which partially covered them. Great white air-bubbles rolled along under these ice decks. Here and there watercress, buttercup leaves and long blades of grass could be seen pressed upward against the transparent ice by the pulsating current. In one pool in the pine woods the floor of the little basin was studded with scarlet partridge berries, surrounded by their rich green leaves.

The view from the crest of the ledges was well worth a harder climb. Mystic Pond is beautiful in itself, but it is made more so by the Fell country, rugged and snow-laden, rising above it. Winchester, with its many-colored cottages sprinkled over the snow, made a pleasing picture. Beyond pond, village, and the Fells, loomed the distant heights upon which the Danvers Asylum showed its gloomy walls. The snow flurries which blurred the distance made the nest of cities along the Charles softer and more picturesque than usual. The ledges are well wooded. Pitch-pines, cedars and a sprinkling of hardwood cover them. Among these trees were crows, a small hawk, a blue jay, two kinglets, two little brown creepers, and nearly a dozen chickadees. The creepers and two of the chickadees were working together. Both pairs of birds signalled each other constantly. If a creeper flew it told its mate, who soon followed, usually flying to the same tree. The chickadees sometimes went to the same tree also, and seemed to be always within forty or fifty feet of the creepers.

From this hill, which used to be called Mt.

Pisgah, I made a bee line for Turkey or One
Pine Hill, in Arlington. Much of the intermediate region is filled with white pines. In one
grove of many hundred large pines, the effects of
the dark green roof, pure white floor and straight
brown columns forming radiating vistas were
impressive, none the less so from the silence and
the cold. From a brier thicket on the edge of
this wood a grouse flew noisily. Near Turkey
Hill was an odd meeting of paths in the snow.
A horse and sled, a man, a large dog, two quail,
a rabbit, and a mouse had all left their prints on
a square rod of snow.

It was the last calendar day of winter. The
sun was going down in wrath. The wind blew
across the top of One Pine Hill impatiently.
One Pine, with its sixty stubs of dead and
broken branches, trembled, and told by its fee-
bleness of the approaching day when One Pine
Hill, successor of Three Pine Hill, shall become
No Pine Hill.

March came in at midnight smiling. The big
yellow moon looked down upon the soft snow
which had fallen since sunset, wrapping the earth
in ermine. I chose Lincoln for my objective
point, and reached it by rail early in the forenoon. The air was keen, very keen, the sky
faintly blue through thin clouds, the sun only a
yellow spot in the south. Leaving the railway

I wound my way back towards Stony Brook, passing through groves of small oaks, meadows full of treacherous pools covered with brittle ice, belts of whispering white-pines, apple orchards and wood-roads leading up hill and down, ending nowhere. Four miles of this wandering brought me to Kendal Green station in Weston, with a record of twenty crows, eighteen chickadees, sixteen tree-sparrows and three blue jays. Every farmhouse seemed to have its two or three large elms, and its one, two or three noisy chickadees. No English sparrows were to be seen. The sleighing throughout the region appeared to be good and the snow in the fields was more than six inches deep on a level. The aspect of the country was much more wintry than it was nearer the coast, yet Lincoln is only thirteen miles northwest of the State House. For two weeks past the pussy willows had been increasing in size and beauty. Some of them had now reached their most attractive state, for when they begin to push out their yellow stamens they lose much of their peculiar charm. Near Kendal Green I found a noble family of these little Quakers. They were large, and closely set on their stems. Within a foot of the tip of one wand were thirty pussies, each measuring from a half to three quarters of an inch in length. Lincoln, judging by the tracks in the snow, is well stocked with rabbits, field mice and skunks. It showed me the first fox track I have seen in Massachusetts this winter. A fox's track resembles closely that of the dog, but it has some marked distinctions. The fox often clips the snow with his toes, thus prolonging his footprint slightly; he also has a longer stride than a dog of the same size, and sets his feet more nearly in a single line. The footprints of the skunk are grouped in fours, and the four prints in each group are very nearly in line ; the first and third being a little to one side, and the second and fourth to the other side, of an imaginary middle line.

Just above Kendal Green station the railway builders have taken a large bite out of a gravelly hillside. The bitten spot faces southeast and is as warm a nook on a windy winter day as could well be found. It is stocked with dried weed stalks, sumacs with their prince's feather-like spikes, and red cedars covered with fruit. As I rounded the corner of the bitten bank, Spring herself stepped out to meet me, for twelve bluebirds rose in a flock and flew into the cedars and apple-trees which surmounted the cutting. It was 1.30 P. M., and as every cloud had vanished from the sky the sunlight brought out the coloring of these beautiful birds with marvelous intensity. It is hard to say which is loveliest, the cerulean flash from their backs, or the chestnut warmth of their round breasts. I watched and listened to these birds for more than an hour. They were joyously happy. They flew, they basked in the sunlight, they went to the orchard and peered into a hole in an apple limb in which many a bluebird has probably been hatched; they hovered all over the cedars, eating their bluish, aromatic fruit; they perched on the ice at the brink of Stony Brook and drank from the rushing water; they pecked at the sumac spikes, they sipped melting snow on the slate roof of the freight house; they swung on the telegraph wires, and they filled the air with their sweet, simple notes. The station - master said some of them had been seen the Wednesday previous. At last I left them unwillingly, and walked down the track which follows Stony Brook towards Waltham. In the swift current between the ice which projected far out from each shore a muskrat was swimming down stream; twice he dived and twice he surged along with the cold flood before I passed him.

THE MINUTE-MAN IN A SNOWDRIFT.

IT is not often that snow-shoes are useful in this part of Massachusetts, but as about sixteen inches of a recent fall remained on the hills when I took my walk on Saturday, March 7, I found snow - shoes not only useful but necessary for cross-country travel. My shoes were made by a neat-fingered farmer in the White Mountains, and are more durable than many of the fancy shoes for sale among athletic goods. A fish-shaped frame of ash with two cross braces is filled with a coarse mesh of rawhide. The foot is secured to this light framework by a leather toe-cap from which straps extend across the top of the instep and around the ankle. The heel is free to rise and fall in walking, while the heel of the snow-shoe is loaded to make it trail upon the snow, thus keeping the toe up and away from snags.

I spent most of Saturday afternoon on the crest of a high hill not far from the Belmont mineral spring. The air was warm and clear, the sunlight intensely bright, and the sky wonderfully blue. Birds were few and far between, and it is possible that many individuals here in the winter have decamped already. Two crows, two chickadees, two brown creepers, six robins, four quail, constituted my list for the day. The robins passed overhead about three o'clock, flying high, fast, and due north. They may not have stopped short of the New Hampshire hills, for which they seemed to be aiming. The quail were feeding on barberries, and judging by their tracks there seemed to have been eight or ten of them at work. A quail's footprint looks like the barb and part of the shaft of an arrow pointing in the direction from which the bird has come. When they hurry, their tracks are run together, forming a continuous line of perpetuated panic. The quail were quite noisy on Saturday, making a harsh call unlike their "bob, bob-white." During the coming week or fortnight the number of kinds of birds near Boston is likely to increase. I have long been hoping to see crossbills, redpoll linnets, siskins, red bellied nuthatches and others of the winter birds, but this is an off year for them. Now I am looking for redwing blackbirds, purple grackles and rusty grackles, song sparrows, swamp sparrows, fox sparrows, purple finches, pewees and other early migrants.

About sunset on Saturday I was in a grove of venerable red cedars. The lower half of the

trees was in shadow, the upper half in sunlight. Below, all seemed cold and dreary : the
unbroken snow, the rough trunks of the trees,
their sombre foliage. Above, all seemed warm
and cheerful : the bright blue sky, the passing
bits of white cloud, the upper branches of the
cedars glowing with golden olive-green. I
sought an open ledge where I could see from
Blue Hill to Monadnock, and watched the sun
sink into a bed of clouds. The after effects of
color were pronounced. Overhead the sky was
cobalt ; low in the east it was pale Prussian
blue ; in the north it was deep orange, and in the
west silvery, with a few dark ragged clouds
shredded over it. After sunset and just before
darkness comes, colors, irrespective of the outlines of the objects to which they belong, stand
out more forcibly than at any other time. This
was noticeable Saturday evening. The red of a
distant steeple was aggressive ; so was the yellow
of some tufts of dead grass waving in the wind,
and so was the russet of the dried leaves on a
grove of oaks or beeches two miles distant.
The sky at that hour was a matchless background for the copper-colored stems of the
willow trees, the bewildering network of descending lines in an elm's branches and twigs ; and
the distant rows of maples marching along an
opposing hilltop with the orange light of the

northern sky burning through them. Mist effects, and glimpses of distances through driving snowflakes are fascinating, because they leave much to the imagination. Views of clear sunset skies, radiant with color, ranks of leafless trees showing black against the snow, peaks of snow growing bluer as night draws on — these also are fascinating, because the eye seems to gain the truth about whatever it rests upon. Everything is clean-cut, sharply outlined against sky or snow, sincere, real, satisfying.

Sunday, the 8th, was as warm and still a day as the month of March is capable of producing. From early morning until late in the afternoon there was not breeze enough to rustle a leaf, much less to cool cheek and eye smarting under the direct and reflected rays of the sun. I took an early train to Bedford and began my walk there, not because of the charms of Bedford, but because the train went no further. Bedford is a pleasant, old-fashioned village, in the midst of a comparatively flat country. Walking through the village I noticed its high-shouldered and many windowed meeting-house, its haughty elms, and its air of ancient respectability. Five miles away, said a weather-worn guide board, is Concord town; so I turned westward, feeling sure that early spring birds must

haunt the home of Thoreau. Just outside of
Bedford streets I sat down on a stone wall to
bask in the warm sunshine. The mercury stood
at 68° in the shade, yet a snowdrift close by was
four and a half feet in depth. The bell of the
old meeting-house was tolling, and distance
made its voice sweet. It sometimes seems as
though church bells attract the birds. In the
perfect stillness of the air I could hear many
bird notes. A yellowhammer was calling persistently from a distant maple; a bluebird sang
in the nearest orchard, and six noisy crows were
flying to and fro in a ploughed field examining
spots of earth left bare by the receding snow.
Presently a flock of three blue jays entered the
orchard and seemed to find satisfactory food in
the apples left on the ground last autumn.

Between Bedford and Concord I saw eleven
more blue jays, a dozen more crows, thirteen
chickadees, five tree-sparrows and the tracks
of a flock of ten quail. There were also many
crow tracks in the snow. They are larger
than those of quail and the print of the long
hind toe is very marked. The feature of the
day was the repeated occurrence of blue jays.
The birds were noisy and restless, and most of
them were moving northward. The country
through which I passed was level and uninter-
esting. Little timber was in sight, and most of

the farms had an air of being mortgaged. Dirty cows and heifers sunned themselves in the barn-yards, multitudes of hens roamed over bare spots around the buildings, and mongrel curs barked from back door-steps.

Before taking an afternoon train back from Concord, I wandered about the town for an hour, admiring its aged shade trees and comfortable homesteads. In front of one of these homesteads a red squirrel was eating buds from the upper branches of the elm. If the British soldier had tried to reach the bridge over Concord River he would have had hard work to get at the "embattled farmer," for snow varying from ten inches to more than two feet in depth blocked the lane leading to the Minute-Man. Only the foot of a crow had trodden the white covering of historic ground, and the silence and loneliness but added to the charm and suggestiveness of the scene. The Old Manse could be seen through the leafless elms, the snow drifted high against its walls. The eager river hurried along under the bridge, bearing away many a raft of ice. The alert figure in bronze stood above the stream gazing through the elm vista at the snow-covered distance. He is emblematic of something more than our national vigilance against political injustice.   Our nation was not formed when his musket was loaded.   He was simply an Anglo-Saxon standing for his rights.   That is what he is to-day, — the spirit of the race.

THE COMING OF THE BIRDS.

THE week between March 8th and 14th was one filled with early spring messages. The air whispered them, and the stems of the willows blushed with joy at what it said. The sun stripped the snow from the earth and found beneath it green grass, buttercup and five-finger leaves and the sage-green velvet of the mullein. Ice moved in the streams and partially melted on the marshes, and its going was hailed with merry music by song-sparrows, bluebirds, and redwing blackbirds.

Not long after sunrise on Thursday, the 12th, I was in the tangle of rose bushes, willows and rushes, which surrounds the West Cambridge brickyards and clay pits. It was a still, warm morning. Birds were singing on every side. They were not chirping pretty fragments of song, but pouring out in all the plenitude of fearless happiness their greeting to home and a new day. Before 8.30 I saw nearly a dozen song sparrows, a bluebird, a tree sparrow, a flock of twenty-six cedar birds, large numbers of crows, and an Acadian owl. My meeting

with the little "saw-whet" within the limits
of Cambridge, and in sight of dozens of passers
on Concord turnpike, was a piece of unusual
luck. He was perched in a large willow about
thirty feet distant from the sidewalk, and ten
feet from the ground. As I jumped the fence
and approached him he stiffened himself, drew
his feathers close to his body, more than half
closed his eyes and pretended to be a speckled
brown and white stump of a limb. As I raised
a broken branch before his face, his big yellow
eyes opened wide, his wings quickly spread and
he fell forward upon them and flapped noiselessly
to a distant tree.

Late on Friday afternoon, while traversing
the marshes between Spy Pond in Arlington
and Fresh Pond in Cambridge, I saw a flock
of seven blackbirds. They seemed to be following up Alewife Brook towards the marshes
between Cambridge and Belmont. They were
beating against a high wind and flying too
high for me to be sure whether they were red-
winged blackbirds or rusty grackles. Early
Saturday morning I set out to find them, and
not long after sunrise I heard the familiar
"cong-ka-ree" of the redwings coming from
a swamp north of Fresh Pond. I saw three,
the one nearest me being a male, whose scarlet
and buff epaulets fairly blazed in the sunlight.

Prolonging my morning walk for some distance I saw five song sparrows, three bluebirds, two herring gulls, four robins, a meadow lark, a pigeon woodpecker, and a pair of sparrow hawks. The latter showed unmistakably by their love-making that they were paired for the season. They were in a grove of lofty hard-wood trees, in the hollow of one of which they have nested for several years.

For my Saturday afternoon walk I chose the belt of rough country north of the Lexington Branch Railway, between Arlington village and Great Meadow in Lexington. Leaving the train at East Lexington, I crossed the lower end of Great Meadow and aimed for the pine-crested ledges to the north and east. On these low-lands I saw two song sparrows and six tree sparrows in company. A blustering and cold wind was blowing, and the birds kept close to cover. The tree sparrows allowed me to come within six or eight feet of them, in preference to flying. In the midst of ploughed and ditched meadow land was a cup-shaped hollow filled with a frozen bog. Red maples grew in it thickly, and under them a group of alders. As I passed this spot, the roaring wind almost led me to ignore a sharp squeak of alarm from a bird which was scratching in the leaves on the edge of the hollow. Fortunately I heard it, and fol-

lowed the bird and its companion until they flew
from bush to bush into a maple. They were
bright iron-rust color on their tails, rumps, and
wings, and their white breasts were thickly
marked with arrowheads of the same pronounced
shade. In size, they outranked an English
sparrow by about one fifth. They were fox
sparrows. In plumage, song, and character,
these sparrows are among the most favored of
American birds.

Leaving the lowlands, I ascended the heavily
wooded ledges, of which Turkey or One Pine
Hill is the best known. Concealed within
them is a deep yet sunny ravine where hepatica
grows, and over which in the tops of lofty pines
crows, hawks, and gray squirrels make their
nests. I was welcomed to this sylvan glen by
a brown rabbit, who permitted me to come
within a yard of him before displaying his cotton
tail in flight. Hepatica was not in bloom, but,
rising between its trilobate leaves of last year's
growth, nearly an inch of new sprout promised
early flowers. From the middle of the dancing
brook at the bottom of the ravine to the stems
of the great pines at its summit, the melting
snow had exposed to view old vegetation, holding new-born life in its protecting arms. In the
brook, hundreds of heads of skunk-cabbage
could be counted. From the overhanging rocks,

the evergreen fronds of four species of ferns
(including *asplenium ebeneum*) nodded in the
breeze. Upon the sunny banks partridge berries and the clustered jewels of the false
solomon's-seal gleamed among green leaves and
brown pine needles. Three kinds of pyrola,
rattlesnake-plantain, pipsissewa, buttercup, and
three club mosses decorated the steep slopes.
On a warm gray face of ledge above, a generous
growth of bearberry spread its lustrous green
and russet leaves to the sky, and close by the
pale corydalis grew in abundance. The recent
growth in some of these plants was marked, par-
ticularly in the buttercup (*R. bulbosus*) and
bearberry. Walking back to Arlington, I saw
a downy woodpecker, a grouse, two golden-
crested kinglets, four chickadees, a dozen
crows, two flocks of blackbirds, including
fully forty birds, three more tree sparrows, a
fat spider, two black and orange caterpillars,
two snow-squalls, and a beautiful golden sunset.
Saturday night was clear and cold, more like a
winter night than one with some claims to the
name of spring.

Sunday, the middle day of March, was bright
and blustering, a sharp contrast to the Sunday
previous, with its heat and strange stillness. I
began my walk at Waverley, and went by way of
Quince Street and Beaver Street to the easterly

slope of Prospect Hill, in Waltham. The roads
were frozen, and the meadows stiff with ice.
Here and there roaring brooks passed under the
road and danced away towards the Charles.
The spaces between them were in some instances
filled by ledgy hills capped and sprinkled with
red cedars, some of which were sturdy old
trees with foliage full of golden-olive light.
From one of the hills came a gay troop of
robins flying in wide circles over the fields.
One of them sang in a timid way the song of
robin's love. It was the first attempt at the
complete song that I had heard this season.
From another ledge, covered with hardwood
trees, eight chickadees deployed across an orchard. Every one of them was saying something merry. On the edge of a meadow seven
bluebirds sat in the low branches of maple-
trees, and dropped one by one to the ground
to pick up food seen by their quick eyes in
the grass. I saw three more bluebirds later
in the day. Near the foot of Prospect Hill, a
flock of nearly a dozen birds, feeding in a yard
among spruces and maples, was found to include
chickadees, brown creepers, and a kinglet. I
saw four brown creepers during the day, one
of which in flying described curves and spirals
in the air which would have made a tumbler
pigeon green with envy. In a sheltered nook

by a spring, a thicket of evergreens, and a brush fence, two fox sparrows popped into view for a moment. Near them a grouse was found in a pine grove.

The eastern side of Prospect Hill holds in its curve a spot of singular beauty. Behind a veil of pine woods lies hidden a rocky amphitheatre, through which flows a sparkling stream of spring water. Dozens of its tiny cascades were framed in moss and ferns. Its worn boulders were partially sheathed in ice, and in many places beds of snow still rested upon its banks and overhung the water. The background of this picture was a steep wall of rock and earth nearly fifty feet in height, overhung by tall oaks, walnut and ash trees, and covered with remnants of snow drifts, mossy boulders and patches of last year's ferns nodding in the wind.

Scrambling up this cliff, I found myself at the summit of a hill justly noted for its wide and varied view. A vast and irregular city seemed to reach from its southeastern foot to the waters of Massachusetts Bay. Far away to the southwest, two large towns could be seen rearing their spires against the sky. They were about in the direction of Westboro' and Milford. The New Hampshire mountains showed to much better advantage than from Arlington Heights, and I could clearly identify the different summits of the Monadnock range. But this was not all. Just to the left of the twin Uncanoonucs was what appeared to be the southern Kearsarge, in Andover, New Hampshire. This peak is seventy-five miles distant, and has an elevation of 2,943 feet. I am less confident that I could distinguish Agamenticus in York, Maine, but a faint blue summit broke the monotonous sky line near the point at which this hill might be seen were it high enough.

THE EQUINOCTIAL ON THE DUNES.

THE dunes of Ipswich in Massachusetts lie in a somewhat secluded and peculiar spot. Facing the open ocean between Plum Island and Coffin's Beach, the Ipswich shore presents a strange aspect to the passing world, seaward, skyward, or landward. It is a rough bit of desert, made into odd shapes by wind, tide, and river. From no point of view is it commonplace.

An early morning train from Boston landed me on March 21 at Ipswich station. Rain fell in a determined way upon the earth, the snowdrifts, and the rushing Ipswich River. In a rickety buggy drawn by a lean horse I started for the dunes. It was a five-mile drive over a rolling glacial plain and wind-swept marsh land. As the sea was neared, the wind became stronger and stronger. The buggy swayed from side to side; the lean horse, stung by rain in front and whip behind, staggered feebly on against the storm; and birds, waves, sand, trees, marsh grass, the face of the water, — everything, in fact, which could move, —

either fled before the gale or writhed under its
blows. At nine o'clock I reached a lonely, storm-
battered house, half concealed among the sand-
hills. The Equinoctial was at its height. It
was an hour when prudence bade one stay in the
house, but when that which makes a man happy
among the rough revelry of Nature said, Go,
give yourself to the storm. The sea could not
be seen from the house, for the dunes stood in
the way, but the wind, the breath of the sea,
told where it lay. The wind was charged with
rain, hail, cutting bits of sand, the odor of brine,
and the roar of the billowy battle beyond the
dunes.

What are the dunes? They are the waves of
the sea perpetuated in sand. They were changing
and growing at that moment, as they are at every
moment when the winds blow. A ridge forty feet
high, eastward of the house, was hurling yellowish sand into the dooryard and against the buildings. From its top could be seen a hollow beyond and then another ridge, from the crest
of which a sand banner waved in the wind.
That ridge surmounted, a broader hollow was
seen beyond, containing lagoons of gleaming
water and thickets of richly colored shrubs and
a few stunted pines. To right, left, and ahead,
other ridges rose like mimic mountains. Some
of them had been cut straight through by

storms, and showed plainly wind stratification on their cut surfaces. Wading through the pools, from which a few black ducks rose and flew swiftly out to sea, I gained the third ridge, which was the highest of the dunes. Beyond was another hollow, then a fourth dune, then a beach strewn with seaweed, shells, and wreckage, and finally half a mile of snowy breakers, boiling and hissing on their rhythmic journey shoreward. At times the eye seemed to reach further out to sea, but at once the rain, foam, and driving cloud-masses closed in on the waves, and sky and ocean were combined in an attempt to overwhelm the dunes. Walking upon the beach was like wrestling with a strong man. Looking through the stinging rain was almost impossible. Not far up the beach was the wreck of a small schooner. It was half buried in the sand and just within reach of the waves. Streaming with rain, my face smarting from the flying sand, and my breath exhausted, I gained the wreck and sought a refuge in its interior.

The wreck's ribs rose high into the air, and a part of her sheathing had not yet been beaten off by gales. The waves struck this wall of plank and sent shiver after shiver through the broken hulk. Inside, the wind had little effect, and the water that came in was that flowing downward from the beach, as great waves broke upon the sand

and then swept round over the wreck's buried
side. Peering through the gaps between the tim-
bers, I looked down into and across a raging
mass of water. It was equal to a shipwreck
without the fear of death. Dozens of herring
gulls, now and then a black-backed gull, and
every few minutes small flocks of black ducks,
flew past athwart the gale. Sometimes a gull
would face the wind and fly against it steadily,
vigorously, yet never advance an inch. The
ducks looked as though they were flying backward, so oddly balanced were they. After
nearly an hour of watching I waded ashore, followed my tracks back across the sand-hills, and
gained a comfortable " stove-side " in the weather-
beaten house. The noonday meal of fat pork,
boiled corned beef, cabbage, clams, soda bis-
cuit, doughnuts, mince pie, and coffee seemed
in some degree a reasonable complement to the
gale.

Early in the afternoon, in company with two
friends, — a bird-watcher and a mouse-hunter, —
I faced the storm again. We walked northward rather than eastward, keeping within the
hollows of the dunes and not climbing to their
windy crests. Rain fell in torrents and in larger
drops than in the morning. It whipped into
foam the pale blue and green pools between the
sand-hills. Gusts of air struck these pools from

ever-varying angles, the cliffs and passes of the
mimic mountains making all manner of currents
and eddies in the wind. Ruffled by these gusts
the pools changed color from moment to moment, sometimes being white with foam and
reflected light from the sky, then varying
through every shade of blue and sea-green to
ultramarine. The coloring in these miniature
valleys was exquisitely beautiful. In some, the
yellow sand, over which lines and ripples of purple sand were laid, curved from every side with
the most graceful lines downward from the
ridges to a single tinted mirror at the centre.
In others, where the valley was broader, lagoons
filled with tiny islands were fringed with vegetation of striking shades. The clumps of sturdy
" poverty grass " (*hudsonia tomentosa*) covered much of the ground, its coloring, while it
was wet by the rain, varying from burnt umber
to madder brown. Over it strayed scalp locks
of pale yellow grasses, restless in the wind.
Next to the pools and under them grew a dense
carpet of cranberry vines, yielding shades of
dark crimson, maroon, and wine color. Lines
of floating cranberries edged these tiny lakes,
or shone like precious stones at their bottom.
Between the lagoons and on their islands dense
thickets of meadow-sweet and leafless wild-rose
bushes formed masses of intense color, the

shades running from rich reds through orange to gleaming yellow. The rain glistening on these warmly tinted stems made them unnaturally brilliant.

On the shores of some of the lagoons, or forming small conical islands in their midst, were white heaps of broken clam-shells. The shells when disturbed seemed to be embedded in fine black soil, like that left by long-extinguished fires. When these shell-heaps were first explored they contained bones of many kinds of fish and birds, including fragments of that extinct bird, the great auk. They also yielded broken pieces of roughly ornamented pottery, bits of copper, and stone implements of the Indians who had made the Ipswich River and its sand-hills one of their principal camping-grounds. This region has given to relic-hunters bushels of arrow-heads, stone knives, and hatchets.

As we approached the largest of the lagoons, which covered several acres, black ducks began to appear, flying in all directions. They rose not only from the large lagoon, but from many smaller pools hidden among the network of dunes. Over a hundred were in the air at once. Crows, too, and gulls joined in the winged stampede caused by our coming. One flock of crows flying towards Cape Ann later in the afternoon numbered eighty-three birds. Our walk ended at Ipswich Light, a small beacon placed on the edge of the dunes as a warning against their treacherous sands. A bit of land near it had been reclaimed from the desert and gave promise of being a garden in a few weeks. The rain was at its fiercest here, and beat upon the lighthouse as though it would wash it from the face of the earth. As the wind blew the sand grass, its long blades whirled around, cutting circles in the sand with their tough tips and edges. These circles could be seen from a long distance, so deeply and clearly were they cut. Sometimes a long blade and a short one whirled on the same root and made concentric circles. The geometrical correctness of these figures made them striking elements in a landscape so chaotic as the dunes in the Equinoctial.

Scattered about over the sand were small star-shaped objects about the size of a silver dollar, and brown in color. They looked at first glance as though they might have been stamped out of thick leather. Whether they were fish, flesh, or plant, was a question not readily answered by a novice. They proved to be a kind of puff-ball, common in such regions as the dunes, and singularly well adapted to life on shifting sands.

Through the long night of the 21st the wind wailed around the house, and the sound of the

waves came up from the sea. Long before sunrise I was awakened by the quacking of domestic ducks in the inlet just in front of my
windows. Fog and a gentle east wind ruled the
morning, and the fog made queer work with
outlines and perspective among the sand-hills.
Not far from the house there once stood a fine
orchard, many of the trees in which had attained
a generous size considering their exposed situa-
tion. But the dunes marked them for destruc-
tion. The greedy sand piled itself around
their roots, rose higher and higher on their
trunks, caught the tips of their lower branches,
dragged them under its cold and deadly
weight, reached up to those higher, and, as the
trees began to pine, hurled itself against their
dry leaves, twigs, and branches, then set to work
to wear away the trunks themselves. Rising
through the fog, these remains seemed like tor-
tured victims reaching out distorted arms for
pity. Only a few of the trees retained branches
having green wood and pliable twigs, and these
were half buried by recent inroads of sand.
They reminded me of the fate of men caught in
quicksands, and drawn down inch by inch to
their death.

Tracks in sand are almost as telling records
as tracks in snow. Skunks had wandered about
over these ridges in force. They do not find

their food among the hills, but on the shore where the carrion of the sea is left by the tide. The ocean edge is usually strewn with dead fish, sea birds, and shell-fish. Around these remnants are to be seen the tracks of gulls and crows, or the birds themselves. That morning the upper air was noisy with crows coming back from their night roost. They soon scattered along the beach, feeding. For some reason the ducks had disappeared from the lagoons. A few flew past up the coast, but the greater part seemed to have already moved northward. It was upon these sand-hills that the Ipswich sparrow was first shot in December, 1868. The bird is much like the grass finch in contour, and in behavior when approached by man. Its coloring is that of the Savannah sparrow, only several shades lighter. During the March migration the Ipswich sparrow is readily to be found among the dunes. Startled by my coming, three of them stopped feeding on the edge of a small, clear lagoon and flew up the steep side of the sand-hill above it. This sand-hill was dotted with clumps of coarse, yellowish grass, the sand itself was a shade paler than the grass, and the sparrows' plumage toned in with both so perfectly that when the birds alighted it was almost impossible to see them. One dropped down behind a bunch of grass, and ran along swiftly with his head pointing forward until he gained the cover of a larger growth of grass, then stopped and raised his head slowly above it, and remained motionless, vigilant.

Crouched among the grass in a hollow I watched him, my glass levelled at his head. Five minutes may have passed before he gave a sharp " chip," ran at full speed down the bank, and flew back to his feeding-ground. Near another pool a dozen or more horned larks were feeding on the wet ground. This bird is one of the most beautiful I know. In the pool, caddis-worms were crawling about in cases made, not of grains of gravel, but of sections of scouring-rush, which they had found to answer all practical purposes. This is an instance of the use of ready-made clothing to oppose to Nature's usual demand for custom-made garments. These caddis-worms were the first water-life which I had seen stirring this spring. Later in the day I saw " Tom Coddies " or " mummichogs " swimming in a ditch, but they are active all winter. Another sign of spring was the track of a white-footed mouse (*hesperomys leucopus*) found by the mouse-hunter on his morning round.

Standing on the crest of one of the dunes next the sea, and looking through the fog across lagoons filled with islands to other dunes of many outlines, varying from pointed peak or bold bluff to long graceful ridge, it was impossible to retain true ideas of size and distance. The proportions of pools, islets, bushes, and cliffs corresponded so closely to those which would have marked lakes, islands, groves, and mountain peaks that, for all the eye could tell, Winnepesaukee and the Franconia Mountains were there in all their beauty. During the forenoon the fog crept back to the sea, the sun came out, and the landscape appeared in new colors and proportions. Lakes shrank to pools, mountains dwindled to sand ridges. The sand itself grew pale, and many of its most brightly colored plants lost their brilliancy as they dried. This was strikingly noticeable in the *hudsonia tomentosa,* which changed from rich brown tones to sage green and gray. Ducks were replaced by numbers of redwing blackbirds, and all day long the " flick, flick, flick, flick, flick " of a pigeon woodpecker rang from a tree on Hog Island.

In the afternoon we rowed across the shallow inlet to the island, which is what geologists call a drumlin, and sailors or farmers a " hog back." It is a gently sloping hill of gravel, whose longer axis is supposed to indicate the direction of the glacier's advance at that point. The length of the island from northwest to southeast is a little

over half a mile, and its height along its backbone
is one hundred and forty feet. A sunny old
farm-house on the low land at the end of the
island nearest Coffin's Beach was pointed out
as the birthplace of Rufus Choate. Beyond it
was a fair view of Essex River, with its gleaming
flats dotted with clam-diggers, Coffin's Beach,
Annisquam Harbor, and the shores of Cape
Ann, made dim and mysterious by the east wind's
veil of haze, a pledge of returning storm. The
view northward across Castle Neck and the
mouths of Ipswich and Rowley rivers to Plum
Island was not only beautiful, but interesting by
reason of the distinctness with which it mapped
the dunes. As line upon line of white-edged
breakers rolled in upon the shore, they seemed to
turn to sand and continue their undulations
across Castle Neck to our inlet. Bits of blue
shone between these sand waves. They were
the mimic lakes of the caddis-worms and the
Ipswich sparrows. Bits of white were on the
sands of the beach and the flats along the
inlet. They were flocks of gulls feeding. So
still was the air that now and then the uncanny
whining of one of these birds came up to us.
Inland the sun made the haze golden instead
of gray, and we could not see many miles.
In Ipswich, Hamilton, and Essex many drum-
lins could be seen, one of which, Heartbreak

Hill, was especially conspicuous. The outlines of these hills seemed restful and placid. The marshes between them were straw-colored, and cut into arabesques by meandering tide rivers of blue.

The stone walls on Hog Island were apparently being swallowed up by the earth. The boulders also seemed to be sinking below the surface. One stone wall had sunk so that its top was almost level with the ground. In the fields at the base of the hill, tunnels of the common field-mice (*arvicola pennsylvanicus*) ran in every direction. The mouse-hunter, in order to prove beyond a doubt that these sturdy mice, and not moles, were responsible for the tunnels, dug one of them out of his cave and produced him, struggling.

At sunset, after our row back to the sand-hills, I climbed the highest dune and took a last look at the singular panorama of blue lagoons, pale yellow ridges, wind-cut bluffs, buried trees, and foaming breakers. It certainly was a unique landscape, and one fascinating for many reasons, but it had something sinister in it. The ocean was covered by a thin fog, the east wind coming from the waves was chilling, and it brought confused sounds of roaring water and shrill-voiced gulls. The sands, forever shifting, seemed treacherous, the sea restless, and the wind which stirred them full of discontent. There are many who might find rest in the restlessness of the sea, the dunes, and the winds. Perhaps my lack of sympathy is hereditary. Rather more than two hundred and fifty years ago a father and son were fishermen upon these treacherous coasts. In the great storm of December 15, 1636, the father was claimed by the ocean as its own. The son gave up the sea and grew corn by the ponds of Chebacco. Before he died he moved out of sight and hearing of the ocean, and for many generations none of his descendants lived within tide-water limits.

THE RENAISSANCE.

THE twenty-fifth of March was the first day of the year which could, without any mental reservation, be called a spring day. I was awakened early by the clamor of English sparrows, the shrill calling of robins, the "creaking" of purple grackles, and the cawing of crows. By eight o'clock, with one who, like myself, had arranged to gauge the season on this bright and beautiful morning, I was on my way behind a willing horse, speeding by Mount Auburn, through the walled fields of Belmont, past Waverley Oaks, and on towards Concord, with Rock Meadow and Beaver Brook on the left, and Arlington Heights and their cedar-crowned ridges on the right. Every breath of fresh, sweet, sparkling air seemed full of new, tingling life. Near Payson Park Lodge a song sparrow was singing. We stopped and listened to it. Every note was well and fully rendered. The bird was, like the day, one of Nature's successes. Just beyond the Oaks, near Beaver Brook Cascade, a flock of a dozen quail flew over us, and on, northward, at a rate of speed which was marvellous. They were flying high enough to clear the tops of the trees. The rush of their wings was like a squall passing through a pine grove.

As we drove slowly between the even rows of willows which make Rock Meadow on the Concord turnpike one of the most charming spots near Cambridge, song sparrows by threes and fours were seen and heard at every lull in the west wind's blowing. Two rusty grackles flew over, alighted in an elm, sounded their quaint notes, and then dropped down into the meadow. A redwing blackbird "ka-reed" from a treetop, and more than a dozen crows revelled in loud cawing, sturdy flying, or rapid walking over the lowlands. Over the hills and far away we drove in the bright sunshine, until, reaching at last the secluded spot we had chosen for our goal, we set out through a narrow, walled lane for the woods.

A muskrat, sunning himself on a stone, seeing us, hurled himself across the lane into and through a puddle, showering spray in every direction, and out of sight under a stone wall beyond. A single junco, the first I had seen this year, rose from a ploughed field, flashed his white tail feathers, and turned his cowled head to watch us. High over a pine-crowned hill a red-shouldered hawk was sailing in small circles,

and with rather nervous flight. Now and then
its discordant mewing came to our ears on the
wings of the wind.

In the orchards bluebirds were singing. We
heard at least ten. They seemed to say, "*Cher-
u-it, cher-u-it,*" and to mean by it something
very pure and endearing. The lane led into
a wooded meadow, crossed by several brooks,
which we examined with interest for signs of
water life. Within half a mile we found one
painted turtle (*chrysemys picta*) and eighteen
speckled tortoises (*nanemys guttatus*). Some
seemed rather feeble, though full of enjoyment
of the warm sunshine. One of the number
had come to an early, sad, and to us mysterious
end. We found his empty shell picked clean
of all soft portions except the tail and a bit of
skin which adhered to it. The shell was unscarred. Neither of us could imagine what
beast or bird could have slain him. The
crime had been committed only a few hours
before, for the shell was still moist. In the
mud on the side of the brook we found an
unfamiliar track. Two five-clawed feet, making
a track as broad as the length of the first joint
of a man's thumb, had been planted side by
side, while several inches in front of them two
smaller feet had made two prints, one of which
was exactly in front of the other. My friend

thought the prints might be those of a young otter. We also found where a muskrat had stepped upon the mud, placing his hind feet so closely together as to make one broad print, dragging meanwhile his tail in such a way as to leave an odd groove in the mud. Flying about in this meadow and the higher woods adjoining it were two kinds of butterflies and a beautiful moth. I also found a partially developed locust.

While watching and admiring these gay survivors of the winter, we heard a brown creeper sing. It was a rare treat. The song is singularly strong, full of meaning and charm, especially when the size of its tiny performer is remembered. A grouse, two tree sparrows, and a downy woodpecker were added to our list towards the middle of the day, and early in the afternoon two chickadees, seemingly mated, were greatly exercised over my friend's excellent mimicry of the " phœbe note " of the male chickadee. The male answered with much vigor, and within less than three feet of the mimic's face. In making this sweet ventriloqual note, the bird throws its head back and opens its beak, quite in the manner of a Christmas-card bird. The only other bird song which we heard was that of the flicker calling energetically to his mate.

The event of the day was the sight of a barred

owl, which we startled into flight in the depths
of a pine grove where snowdrifts still lingered.
Although close watch was kept for frogs or piping hylas, none were seen or heard. Our surprise was great, however, to see a large woodchuck run clumsily through an oak grove, and
turn to watch us from the mouth of his hole.
He was very thin, and probably correspondingly
hungry after his long winter nap. We saw two
gray squirrels, but no red squirrels or chipmunks.
At the base of a boulder, in a moist wood, lay
a garter snake. I caught him, and found his
forked tongue, bright, defiant eyes, and tightly
entwining folds all in the best possible working
order. Near the end of our walk we found a
grass-grown ants' nest, formed of light soil piled
into a conical heap a foot and a half high. Not
thinking it possible that the hill was tenanted, I
knocked away part of its top. Instantly, en-
raged red ants came from the hidden chambers
of their fortress, and in a sluggish way sought
the intruder. I replaced the earth and mentally
begged the ants' pardon.

It was evening when we reëntered Cambridge
streets, well pleased with having seen eighteen
kinds of birds, three kinds of mammals, two
species of turtles, one snake, three species of
butterflies or moths, and at least five other kinds
of insects.

THE VESPER SONG OF THE WOODCOCK.

Easter Sunday fell this year on March 29th, and the joyous voices of white-robed choir boys made for the cities almost as sweet and praiseful music as the children of the woods were making in Nature's own sanctuaries. On the afternoon of the day before Easter, I went to the ravine between Arlington and Lexington where hepatica grows. Walking from Arlington over the ridges near One Pine Hill, I heard frogs for the first time this year. Two kinds were singing, the shrill-voiced piping hylas (*hyla Pickeringii*) and the wood frogs (*rana sylvatica*). The latter at this season make a sound which recalls the thrumming of loosely strung banjo strings. The combined notes formed an effective background of sound to the rollicsome singing of song sparrows, tree sparrows, and red-winged blackbirds, and the love-music of the mated bluebirds.

Wishing to capture a wood frog and make sure of his identity, I remained for many minutes motionless on a stone in the middle of a shallow pool in the swamp. On my approach

every frog had gone to the bottom and hidden
in the leaves and mud. The pool was lined
with many layers of brown leaves, most of which
preserved their outlines and told their names.
Across them twigs and branches had fallen, and
bits of lichen and moss had sunk there, too.
Many specks were floating in the water. They
seemed to move, some one way, some another.
They were alive. Bending closer over the
water, I watched them attentively. Some moved
quite evenly, others hitched across the pool by a
series of jerky advances. There were lively red
ones among them, contrasting with the darker,
duller ones. Some were so minute that they
could be seen only as a ray of light pierced the
pool. As minutes passed and no frog moved, I
grew weary and rose. Instantly a frog kicked
among the leaves and mud, betraying by motion
what his color had protected. A second later I
had him, feebly squirming in my pocket.

North of One Pine Hill a flock of thirty or
more birds were feeding in a stubble field.
They were juncos and tree sparrows, in about
equal numbers. The juncos did not say where
they had been all winter. Only just out of my
sight, perhaps, all the time. At five o'clock the
ravine was reached. It was full of shadows,
and the raw east wind had piled masses of cloud
across the sky, making the sun's light pale and

uncertain. At the masthead of a leafless red
maple sat a gray squirrel, " budding." Foolish
thing, he sat still, thinking himself safe, while
he was really the most conspicuous object in the
ravine. Pounding upon the tree had no effect
on him. Search for hepaticas revealed no
flowers, and I did not find any until a trip to
the Middlesex Fells on April 5th. The skunk-
cabbage flowers were losing their beauty, yet the
snow was still abundant in dark corners in the
woods. Ten minutes in the chilly ravine was
enough. A grouse startled me with her noisy
flight as I left the gloom. From every hilltop
crows were calling lustily. They were restless,
and seemed moved by a common impulse.
Reaching a high ledge, I watched them. About
thirty were in sight in the tops of tall pines.
Gradually they drew together on the next ridge
to the north, about half a mile from me. One
by one they dropped down into the woods out
of sight. At last but two remained, still cawing.
Then they became silent, and finally they also
sank beneath the surface of the woods, and
nothing more was heard of them. They were
like sparks in the ashes, going out one by one.
At this moment the sun, which had been sinking
behind stormy-looking rags of clouds, disappeared behind the rounded shoulder of Wachusett. Then the sky dressed itself in gay colors,

and the farewell to the day was full of splendor.
Wachusett, distant and pale blue, was flanked
by two of the Lexington ridges heavily grown
with pines. The mountain and its two dark
guardians stood out sharply against a background
of the richest orange, deepening at the horizon
to red. Above the mountain the sky was clear
yellow until it reached a bank of slaty-blue
cloud. The sunlight piercing this cloud bank
flecked it with rose color, while drifting bits of
cloud falling against the orange became bright
like gold. Thanks to this gorgeous sunset, I
lingered on the hill until darkness pervaded the
woods. Then I ran down through a grove of
oaks and came out in a damp meadow completely surrounded by tall trees. The last song
sparrow was singing good night. Across the
west only a single band of orange light remained.
In the zenith stars were beginning to shine. A
strange cry came from the meadow grass. It
recalled the night hawk's squawk, softened by
distance. Again and again it came: "N'yah,"
then a pause, then "n'yah" again, and so on,
until this had been uttered a dozen times. I
drew nearer the spot from which this odd call
came. Perhaps it was a frog of some kind; perhaps a bird of the swamp. The sound ceased,
but the next moment there seemed to be a musical ringing in my ears which rapidly grew more

distinct, and then came clearly from the upper
air, but from a point swiftly changing, apparently revolving. I fixed my mind intently
upon the sound. It was a series of single musical notes uttered rapidly by some creature flying swiftly in an immense circle high over the
meadow. It seemed as though the sky were a
vast vaulted whispering gallery under whose
dark blue dome a singing reed was being whirled
round and round, dropping sweet bits of sound
as it sped through the air. As I listened breath-
lessly, this sound was smoothly changed into
another. The creature was descending: its
notes fell more slowly but more distinctly; they
were sweeter, rounder, more liquid. They came
down, down, and then ceased, quenched in the
damp grass. Almost at once, however, the
" n'yah " began again at the same point in the
meadow where it had been made before. This
entire performance was repeated several times.
The last time the nasal call was given twenty-
four times and the aërial part was omitted.
The performer was satisfied for the night. As
he closed, the bells in Arlington struck seven.

Those who know the plump and meditative
woodcock, gazing by the hour together down the
line of his bill into black mud, will wonder with
me that his courtship can arouse him to such
airy fairy efforts, and at so romantic an hour.

A TRIP TO HIGHLAND LIGHT.

THE morning of the first of April dawned like an Easter Sunday. The sky was clear, the sun warm, the air soft and full of the smell of spring. Taking the nine o'clock train from the Old Colony Station we rolled swiftly over the Quincy-Braintree levels with their wandering brooks and flooded swamps, down towards the sandy Cape country. At Bridgewater the train turned toward the east, and by eleven we passed the head of Buzzard's Bay, where the Cape Cod Canal is some day to be cut through, and entered upon the territory of the real Cape. The railway follows the inner curve of the Cape, the rounded cheek of Cape Cod Bay. At Sandwich, where we saw the melancholy and deserted buildings of the once prosperous glass works, we began to gain glimpses of dark blue water, with pale sand hills lining its shores.

As we passed Barnstable and Yarmouth these momentary off-looks to the bay became more frequent. Between them, as we hurried through patches of low woods, we surprised anglers making the first cast of the newly opened season in

the sluggish brooks or small ponds which make
this region famous for its trout. Brewster,
Orleans, Eastham, and Wellfleet were traversed
one by one, the train hitching to the left mile by
mile until from pointing southeast it pointed east,
then northeast, and finally north. We passed
cranberry bogs by dozens; stunted pine forests
scorched by the railway fires; windmills —
some old and full of Dutch dignity, many new
and bristling with Yankee ingenuity; flocks of
blackbirds on the flat hay-fields; clouds of dry
sand rising from the track; views across the
blue bay of blue skies and bluer shores reaching
up to the mainland westward and northward.

By a little after midday our eyes had spanned
the placid inner waters of the bay and seen the
long curving shore of Truro and Provincetown,
its white hills and low cliffs flashing almost like
chalk in the strong sunlight. Passing Wellfleet, — a large and busy-looking village, — we
soon gained a narrower part of the Cape and
began to point northwest instead of north,
seeing sand-hills first on one side, then on
the other. Truro is a long township, a block
set on end in this pile of Cape republics.
First came South Truro, then Truro, then a
mile or two of bluffs along the bay shore with
swift visions of feeding herring gulls on the flats,
and forests of poles rising from the blue water,

marking the fish traps of the deluded fishermen whose mackerel fleet has been swept from the sea by this sunken fleet of seine poles. Finally, North Truro was gained, four hours from Boston, and 114 miles by schedule. The bay was at our feet, with Barnstable, Plymouth, and Norfolk shores for its setting. There was the train running away to Provincetown between white sand walls, pointing toward Boston, yet increasing its sand trail from it. Eastward there was a straight white road leading over low sand ridges and broad sand levels up to a tall white lighthouse a mile and a half away. It was Highland Light, holding its great lenses high above the Atlantic, and casting its message of warning or welcome over many a wide league of restless water. The process of hauling a well-loaded carryall through even a short mile and a half of deep sand is painful for horse and trying to half-starved traveller. Both rejoice when such a ride is over.

At three o'clock we were standing at the foot of Highland Light, gazing on the novel landscape which surrounds it. Toward the east the limitless ocean filled the eye. Half a dozen sails were in sight, but no covey of mackerelmen dotted the sea as in the days of Thoreau. The spot where we were standing was the storm-eaten margin of a cliff about 150 feet in height. The cliff is not rock, but sand and clay sur-

mounted by a tough layer of sod. As years
roll by the cliff is eroded, a little by the sea,
more by the ceaseless winds and frequent falling
rains. The ruins of the cliffs lie at their feet.
First masses of clay formed into mimic mountain
spurs and buttress ridges, then heaps of white
sand covered with coarse grass, finally, next the
sea, the broad steep beach which looks as hard
as marble, but when tested offers only soft and
uncertain support to the foot. The clay débris
is full of odd effects of color. White, gray, yellow, orange, lead color, and black, burning in
sunlight or crossed by heavy shadows, blend into
combinations worthy of the Yellowstone region.
On the upper edge of the cliffs close to the lighthouse a colony of bank swallows have lived
through many generations of both men and birds.
Their burrows aid the work of erosion. Looking either up or down the Atlantic shore the
cliffs could be seen extending in uneven array
above the beach. Southward they were broken
in places where narrow valleys ran inland,
reaching sometimes nearly across the Cape.
Almost the whole of Truro south of the lighthouse is composed of sandhills well sodded or
grown with stunted pitch-pines or oaks. The
intervening valleys or interrupted hollows sometimes contain tide rivers, but are more frequently dry. The hills are low, but as their

pigmy forests have the general effect of large
trees, the observer is constantly deceived as to
proportions and distances. Many times during
my stay I was startled to see an apparently
gigantic man or colossal quadruped come into
view upon the brow of a hill which my eyes had
told me was a mile or two distant. In driving
or walking, spaces were covered so much more
quickly than sight alone led me to expect, that I
felt as though my legs must be the owners of
the seven-league boots of old. Looking westward from the lighthouse, the charm of the
view was not in the foreground of undulating
pasture thickly grown with reindeer moss and
tussocks of brown *hudsonia*, but in the distance. Cape Cod Bay has that lovely contour, that great curve of sand enclosing a mass
of placid blue water, which makes a small bay
a singularly attractive part of a sea picture.
From Highland Light that day the bay seemed
full of repose, ignorant of storm.

Northward the shores of ocean and bay curved
away from the east as though the storm winds had
bent the end of the Cape round into the bay.
Inside of this bent end lay Provincetown, its
many windows flashing back the sunlight, and
its several spires standing out clearly against the
blue background. Between Provincetown and
the ocean are dunes, not grass and lichen-grown

hills, but dunes like those at Ipswich beach, shifting, treacherous, menacing. The sunlight lay upon them as upon snow banks.

Taking a sturdy Cape horse, unterrified by sandy roads or cross-country jaunts, we set out by a trail back of the cliffs for the picturesque country between Highland Light and Province-town. In a hollow behind the cliffs lay a life-saving station with its chain of telephone poles running from it both up and down the coast, and its sentry box perched upon the crest of the sandhill. From a dry field near it an Ipswich sparrow rose, flew a couple of rods, dropped beside a bunch of *hudsonia*, and then ran swiftly away behind its cover. Presently its whitish head appeared amid the grass at a dis-tance and remained motionless but watchful. Our trail ascended a slope and led into a forest of pigmy pitch-pines. They were about six feet high on an average, yet were said to be twenty years old. A flock of forty or fifty gold-finches sang and fed among them. Descending into a broad, level meadow lying just inside the cliffs, which, by this time, were becoming more dunes than cliffs, we found that a fire started intentionally among the coarse grass of the meadow had spread to the low pines and bushes on the sides of the hills. As the wind was east the smoke blew into and across the meadow,

obscuring the view of the dunes in front of us. No
effort of mind or eyesight could make those dunes
appear like anything smaller than mountains two
thousand feet or more in height, and seven or eight
miles distant. Even when some men appeared
upon the nearer ridges and fought the fire, it
was easier to imagine them giants than to reduce
the dunes to their proper proportions.

This meadow was alive with birds. Meadow
larks, which are not larks but starlings, sang
their sweet lament from every acre. With them
were handsome redwing blackbirds, more noisy
but less shy. The starlings rose at long distances and, spreading their tails into white-edged
fans, let their wings quiver and then sailed
away, often over a ridge and out of sight. In
giving his plaintive song the starling stops feeding, raises his head above the grass and shows
to perfection his yellow breast and its bold
black crescent. Song sparrows were on every
side, and crows and gulls rose and fell behind
the sandhills, where they were probably in sole
possession of the ocean's edge with its wealth of
seaweed and sea offal.

After winding through more than a mile of
meadow the road bent sharply to the left and
passed through a crooked gap in the hills into
a sandy amphitheatre several acres in extent.
Here, surrounded by high grass-clad slopes, was

a picture of rural security and comfort. An old-fashioned farmhouse, in the midst of drooping willows, barns, sheds, cattle-yards, and fruit trees, stood near the sunny end of the hollow. At the eastern end was a large pool, thickly grown with stiff, interlacing bushes which rose from the water in the manner of the button-ball bushes. Around the farm buildings were cows, a bull with a large ring in his nose, hens, ducks, and turkeys. Around the pool were song sparrows, tree sparrows, yellow-rumped warblers, crow blackbirds, and redwings. The air was full of their music and the clamor of the barnyard. The spot gave one the feeling that it must have a history. Indians, smugglers, pirates, patriot conspirators, exiled regicides, might one or all have made this nook a place of refuge. The oasis in the desert is seen from afar; this spot of life was hidden in the bosom of the sandhills.

While I was thinking thus the heavens suddenly gave out an unearthly sound ; a drove of celestial jackasses, all braying at once, seemed coming afar from the sun's pastures. Shading my eyes, I discovered a multitude of dark specks connected like a chain, and advancing across the sky with a swaying, undulatory motion. They were wild geese flying a little north of east, and within three hundred feet of the ground. The farmer's dog barked vehemently at them. A

shot rang out from behind the sandhills. The
line of honking migrants wavered, but none
fell. Just as they disappeared a second flock
came within view and hearing in the west, and
passed over us in the invisible wake left by the
first. They seemed to be searching for a place
to rest. The two flocks contained at least
ninety-five birds. Walking round the little
bush-grown pond we listened entranced to the
medley music of the tree sparrows and their
companions. The yellow-rumped warblers were
probably birds which had wintered on the Cape,
just as some others have spent this winter in
Arlington, not far from Mystic Ponds.

The farmer asked us to enter his cottage and
see his collection of Indian stone relics picked
up by him on the slopes and fields above the
pool. We did so and found that he had gathered
several hundred arrow and spear heads, cutting
tools, hammers, bits of wampum and what he
called fish-net sinkers. He took us to the field
west of the pond and home acre, and bade us
search with him for more relics. At the end
of twenty minutes he had aided us in finding
two or three arrowheads, several fragments showing clear indications of having been chipped,
and one sinker. In this field a flock of thirty or
forty horned larks were feeding; they rose and
flew, circled and came down again within fifty

yards of us. I, having failed to find even a broken arrowhead, felt inclined to suspect the larks of hiding them from me, as they tripped about over the ploughed land.

Resuming our places in the carryall, we drove to the edge of a sand slope overlooking the broad meadow between us and Provincetown Harbor.

The sunset hour was near and the bay flashed fire from a million waves. Provincetown, only a few miles away, looked warm and cosy on its neutral ground between pale dunes and blue waters. It would seem less snug in an easterly gale in mid-winter. A broad placid sheet of fresh water lay between the sandhills and the bay shore. It is called the Eel-pond. It made a fair mirror for sunset lights.

We drove home over the moors, as I felt like calling the wastes of undulating lichen-grown sand which formed the middle of the Cape at this point. The horse sped along regardless of roads, but keeping a sharp watch for the numerous holes dug in the sand by recent generations of hunters, who half bury themselves on this plateau at the fortunate times when the golden plover are passing on their hemispherical migration. The horse's feet crunched the reindeer moss, and knocked dust from the *hudsonia* or poverty grass, and pollen from the flowers of the *corema*. Presently we found in the tableland two deep bowl-shaped hollows where twin icebergs had grounded side by side in the great ice age and met their melting death. Upon the narrow ridge between these "sink-holes" was a grave. Years ago a fisherman died of smallpox, and his body was placed there. A stranger burial spot one seldom sees. A mile further on we passed a lonely poplar tree which marks — not a man's grave, but the grave of a home. All trace of the house has gone, but mossgrown roads, a few broken bricks and the sentinel tree bear passing witness to a forgotten fireside; a spot from which a fisherman went out day by day, and where an anxious heart beat for him in storms and perhaps mourned for him at last when his boat went down in the black waters off Race Point. Not far from this forsaken acre is a sink-hole of unusual depth. The local name for it is full of color, — it is "Hell's Bottom." In spite of this name the pines which line the slopes of the hollow flourish and are tall, and the pool of sweet water at its centre is a favorite resort for birds, the holy-crossbill included. Passing it, we saw above pygmy pines the pallid gleam of the Highland Light struggling with the glow of sunset. A wide valley seemed to separate us from the light, and the white tower seemed three hundred feet or more in height, but our Pegasus drew us over the valley in five minutes, and the light shrank to its proper size as we drew near.

About eight o'clock I was seated on the iron steps at the foot of the great kerosene torch which stands inside the crumpled lenses of the Highland light. The lamp roared in its giant chimney. Prismatic colors swam through the lenses. The keepers told strange stories of storms, freaks of lightning, the trembling of their white tower in the gales, and the fate of birds which hurled themselves against the heavy glass of the outer windows of the tower. The base of the lantern and many parts of the interior and exterior of the lighthouse are scarred by lightning. Once three ducks struck and shivered into splinters one of the thick panes of glass in the tower and fell dead and mangled at the foot of the lantern. The keeper said the sound of their striking was like the report of a gun. Outside those windows, flashing with light, all seemed intense darkness, — a gloom filled perhaps with fluttering birds or the mingled thoughts of those upon the ocean who watched from afar the great white light of the Truro sands.

At sunrise on the morning of the second of April, I stood shivering in the chilly air, under the lee of a wrecked windmill not far from the lighthouse. The windmill has lost its wings, and storms have beaten holes in its sides. Half buried in the sand and sod lies one of its grooved mill-stones. Half of the other forms the front doorstep of a house near by. The mill was a kind giant in its time, but being too big to be set up in a bric-a-brac shop in town like its fussy, fairy neighbor the farmer's flax wheel, it is doomed to mingle with the shifting sand and be whirled away by the winds it once made labor.

The sun had come up clear from the ocean. The east wind had an edge both keen and cold. Provincetown lay white and sparkling in the barb of the Cape. Song sparrows, robins, and meadow larks sang joyously. A wicked shrike sat on a stone on the hillside and poured out a jangling mixture of bluebird and brown thrush notes while it watched for victims from among the song sparrows. He never will sing his siren song to another sunrise. Through the pine woods, where skunk tracks dotted the sand patches, and down through a hollow to the beach we strolled before breakfast. Although the hollow was a deep one, we had to slide down fifty feet of soft cliff face before reaching the grassy upper beach, which in turn was several feet above the tide-washed sands. The beach is very soft, and walking upon it is laborious. The cliffs are not as picturesque from below as from above, and they reflect the sunlight disagreeably in early morning. A dead skate, the half feathered skeleton of a kittiwake gull, and a ripe banana constituted nearly the whole of the objects

of interest on the shore. The banana had a remarkably rich flavor, thanks perhaps to its sea
bath. Twenty crows retreated down the beach
ahead of us. They live well and grow fat on the
harvest of death cast up by the waves. We left
the shore at the life-saving station where mortar
drill had just been performed. A man on a
mast set in the sand has the life line fired to
him, he hauls out the breeches-buoy, and an imaginary shipwrecked crew is sent ashore across
imaginary breakers. The station was as neat,
clean and shining as a flagship, and more comfortable by far than most New England farmhouses.

Later in the forenoon we drove for three
hours through Truro and South Truro, seeing
many quaint cottages; dwarf apple orchards reminding me of Thoreau's description of them;
a tide river in which a man was prodding at
random for eels and occasionally bringing one
out squirming on his trident; thousands of pitch-
pine trees planted by hand in rows; a sunny
hillside covered with oaks, checkerberry plants
and arbutus, the latter bearing the first flowers
of the year; and a black snake dozing in the
sand by the wayside. He, being heavy with
winter slumber, was caught, measured, and found
to lie four feet four inches without stretching.
His teeth were long and sharp. Being given

his freedom unhurt he rewarded us by some brilliant tree climbing, during which he glided up a trunk, in and out among branches, and along limbs from tree to tree. I hope he will do no harm during the new term of life which we gave him.

A little after two o'clock we said adieu to North Truro, the fair lighthouse, the cliffs, the heaving Atlantic, and the plaintive starlings. As we rolled homeward along the bay shore hundreds of black ducks flew, swam, or sat motionless upon the quiet water. Gulls by scores fed on the bars or frolicked in the sky. Clouds gathered, the air grew colder, and by midnight Massachusetts was in the midst of one of the fiercest storms of the year.

MONDAY, the 6th of April, found me, with a friend who lives close to nature's heart, floating down the current of Musketaquid. We launched a light Rushton boat at the feet of the Minute-Man, and were swept past him, by the battle-ground, in the tide and through the eddies which Thoreau knew so well and has made immortal. On that morning bright with sunshine yet cold with the breath of snowbanks on Wachusett, it was Thoreau's spirit more than that of the fight-ing farmers or fanciful Hawthorne which seemed to rule the Old Manse ground, the ancient trees along the water's edge, the swirling river, the singing blackbirds, and the landscape of willows, hills, and distant woods. As we were taking out the boat from its house, a downy woodpecker drummed for his mate's enjoyment on the sound-ing branches and trunk of a dead tree at the water's edge. He made three different tones on his drum. A white-bellied nuthatch was going from tree to tree calling loudly. His home of last year had been cut down, and he seemed to

be searching for it. A pair of chickadees passed
by and exchanged greetings with the nuthatch.
Song sparrows in all directions were singing.
Now and then the wild note of a cowbird and
the more distant and plaintive call of a meadow
starling came to our ears. Robins were abundant and noisy.

As our boat floated down the river and turned
a bend towards the arched stone bridge I glanced
back and saw a man with a gun standing on a
ledge above us. I opened my lips to call my
friend's attention to him, when a second glance
showed me that it was the Minute-Man, secure
on his pedestal and not climbing over the nearer
rocks, as he seemed to be. The current under
the bridge was very strong, and for the gentle
Musketaquid, very swift. It required dexterous
paddling to keep a straight course through the
central arch. Beyond the bridge the river lost
itself in flooded meadows. To one familiar with
its rightful banks, a bunch of willows, an elm
and a maple or two told the secret of its course.
But to me it seemed that we were entering a
beautiful lake, which promised to grow wider
and fairer the longer we sailed upon it. Comfortable farmhouses stood upon the higher
ground and looked down at the unruly stream.
Perhaps they recalled the days before the Lowell
dams, when the river was a friend and not a

tyrant to their fair intervales. Along the sheltered furrows in the ploughed fields and against
the cold side of stone walls ribbons of white
snow lay in hiding from the sun. Even in the
streets of Concord we had seen good-sized drifts,
and piles under roof angles. The storm of the
Friday previous, which along the coast brought
rain, had turned to snow here, while further inland many inches of snow had fallen, blocking
roads and breaking wires. The west wind blowing across this wintry stretch of country came
to us well whetted.

From one sloping field it brought us the medley music of a flock of over sixty redwings. As
we listened to the distant choir a rich undercurrent of sound came to us. " Wild geese," I ex-
claimed. My friend shook his head doubtfully,
but paddled ashore to see whether blackbirds
really composed the whole orchestra. We found
them on a patch of high meadow, some in the
trees singing, others on the ground feeding. All
rose and whirled like a puff of burnt paper in
the breeze. Then they settled again, and the
deeper notes in their medley came to us once
more like the far-off honking of geese. Then we
floated on by meadow and brier patch ; thickets
of birch in which the faint spring tints were beginning to grow clearer and stronger ; ploughed
fields over which juncos flashed their white V's ;

bunches of pitch-pines almost as rich as savins in their olive-green coloring; ancient orchards in which respectable families of bluebirds still reside untroubled by the emigrant sparrow; single graceful elms on whose finger tips dangled the gray purses of last year's orioles; fringes of willows bearing their pussies, a few of which showed their yellow stamens just projecting; and maples on whose highest twigs balanced the resident redwings, running over with rippling laughter. My friend spoke of a theory that all bird music is imitative of the sounds best known to the species, and said that the notes of the redwings seemed to bear out this pretty hypothesis, having the sound of water running through their sweet measures.

Gliding across a placid bay in the meadow we came to a wooded shore where a noble oak had just been slain. We landed, and kneeling by its stump counted the year rings. At first it had grown slowly, its young life trembling in the balance; then it gained strength, and the rings were broader and more firmly marked; sometimes narrower ones suggested years of drought; then as our count rose to a hundred, the rings grew closer and closer, as though life passed by very fast in those years. In all, the oak must have lived one hundred and twenty-five years, and have heard the echo of those musket shots which

marked the dawn of Independence, the sunrise
guns of American Freedom. My friend looked
very grave when he saw that this tree was gone.
It had been a landmark, not only on the shore
of Musketaquid, but on the shore of his life, of
which a precious part had been spent on this
river of flooded meadows. Above the oak rose
a bold headland crowned with plumelike pines.
It was Ball's Hill, which Thoreau called "the
St. Ann's of Concord." We sought the top and
looked down upon the fair picture below us.
Great Meadows, the "broad moccasin print,"
was one rippling lake, dotted with islands or
single trees. The river, from the stone arch
bridge, just passed, down to Carlisle bridge with
its wooden piers, had merged its life in this
blue archipelago. The distant tower of Bedford
church recalled my melting walk of a month ago,
when over the snowdrifts the sun of March had
nearly burned my eyes out and quite scorched
the skin from my lips and cheeks. Early spring
in Massachusetts is a crab-like thing, but it has
its charms. In a ploughed field behind the bluff,
we found fox tracks, and under a lofty pine,
pellets of mouse hair, which some owl (or crow
perhaps) had cast from its mouth undigested.

Taking boat once more we wound in and out
along the northern shore. Here, fox sparrows
scratched in the bushes and paused surprised at

the silent monster slipping past them on the lake. There, a shy grouse with ruff wide spread watched us a moment from beneath a proud oak's shade, and then tiptoed away cackling her alarm until the shelter of the great boll gave her a chance to fly. Above, a red-shouldered hawk mewed, and glass in hand we saw him and his mate rise hundreds of feet into the sky, until one was lost in spinning motes of light, and the other, setting her wings, sped down the chute of sky miles away in the northeast. At last, best of all, on the eastern edge of the meadows several snow-white specks were seen upon the water. " Sheldrakes," whispered my companion. They were a quarter of a mile away, but seemed to have seen or heard us, for they were restless. Several times one of the males rose in the water and flapped his wings. Then all took wing and made four or five spirals in the air, ending by disappearing behind a distant growth of birches. " There is a pond in there," said my friend, " with flooded meadows which lead to it." Keeping perfect silence we paddled swiftly across the dancing water to the opposite shore. There the groves opened for us, and a narrow belt of shallows led into an inner meadow. The ducks were not in it. Crossing it, another opening was found leading to a third lake. As we entered this strait I caught an alder bough, and held the boat fast, for not more than two hundred yards from us were the five ducks floating tranquilly in the sheltered lagoon. So silent had been our approach, that although the wind was behind us, the ducks did not suspect our coming. Our glasses made the beautiful creatures seem only a few rods distant, and we watched them closely. One of them was a black or dusky duck, the most abundant species at this season. The other four were mergansers, called also goosanders, fish ducks, or sheldrakes. Two were males, two females; the drakes had lustrous bottle-green heads, and bodies which appeared snowy white. They were enjoying the sunlight, and drifting along slightly with the wind. The black duck kept with them, yet a little apart, — a duck, yet not one of the family. They preened themselves, and soft white feathers floated lightly away upon the ripples. When we had watched long enough, a blow upon the gunwale alarmed the flock. They swam a few feet, first one way, then another. Every motion showed alertness. A second sound booming across the water started them. Their wings dashed the waves into foaming furrows several feet long; then with steady flight they rose in a long diagonal and passed out of sight behind the birches. But only four flew. Sweeping the water with our glasses we discovered the black duck still floating upon its surface. We pushed the boat forward into the lagoon, and the moment he located the danger he rose without a splash and was gone.

Rowing back to the Carlisle side we found a snug corner by a jolly little brook which danced across a pasture down to a meadow, between the rubble walls of an ancient sluice, through the pine woods and into Great Meadows. Over the brook stood an oak; in the oak sat a bluebird; from the bluebird's inmost soul poured the sweetest of bird music, and, wonderful to relate, this music as it fell upon the air turned into goldfinches which undulated over the pasture, finally rested upon the oak and added their songs to the general joy of the occasion. It may be said by harsh commentators that goldfinches never could have been made out of bluebirds' music. Then the burden is on them to prove where the goldfinches come from, for to our eyes they came from the air, which had nothing in it except the song of the bluebird. After lunch and a wonderful concert in which the bluebird sang the solo and the goldfinches did everything else to make it perfect, we examined the ancient sluice. The stone work was rough and without cement. The dam was of earth and from it grew several oaks, one of which may have taken root fifty years ago. As we mused about the dam and its history, a broad-winged,

bluish-gray bird nearly as large as an eagle
sailed swiftly over the meadow. Its course was
low, only a foot or two above the grass, and as
waving from side to side as the letter S. It was
a marsh hawk sweeping the low lands for mice
and frogs. As we walked across the grass he
had been inspecting, we found it dotted with
small piles of fresh earth apparently thrown up
by some burrowing animal working from beneath
the sod. There were also scores of runways or
grooved passages under the matted grass. In
places our feet sank into subterranean chambers,
and in fact the whole field seemed to have been
honeycombed by moles, or meadow mice (*ar-*
vicola pennsylvanicus). The harrier was not
the only bird interested in this field of mice.
Under almost every one of nearly a dozen old
apple trees growing near by we found " owl pellets," the egg-shaped masses of undigested fur,
feathers, teeth and bones which owls habitually
eject from their mouths when well fed.

A quarter of a mile farther on we came to a
stubble field near the banks of Great Meadows.
A stubble field, with a stone wall and a fringe
of bushes round it, is a fine place for migrating
sparrows. Fully a hundred birds were feeding
in this field or singing in the trees which bor-
dered it. They were fox sparrows and juncos,
and it would be impossible to say which were in

the majority. We crept up to them gradually
until all had retreated to the trees at one corner
of the field. Then we merged ourselves in the
stone wall and its brambles and bushes, and remained motionless. One by one the birds drew
nearer. I imitated the shrill singing of a canary.
They began to sing, and the more distant birds
flew boldly over us and into the weeds in the
field. Soon the air was full of them, passing
close to our heads. When they were settled, we
crossed the wall and crawled along behind it
until we were within ten feet of some of the fox
sparrows. These we watched through the cracks
in the wall, and saw them scratch with both feet
in the earth and dry leaves. A hen scratches
with one foot at a time. These birds hitch back-
wards on both feet, twitching their wings at the
same moment and moving both feet together,
although not often exactly side by side. A few
of them sang their full song close by us. It is a
wonderful performance, full of strength, variety
and brilliancy. When the hermit thrush sings
I feel as though the pine forest had been trans-
formed into a cathedral, in which the power of an
organ or the rich voice of a contralto singer was
bringing out the essence of the mass. When
the fox sparrow sings, the effect is entirely different. The quality of the music seems joyous,
not pathetic: that of the grand piano rather than

of the organ ; that of the dance and sunlight
rather than that of vespers. As a maker of
brilliant, vivacious music the fox sparrow stands
among the first. It deserves a place in the list
of the ten finest New England bird singers. In
voice, costume and manners the bird betrays
noble birth. It is a pity that it does not nest
within the limits of our country.

Tearing ourselves away from the sparrows, we
returned to our boat. On the bits of driftwood
lining the shore I found multitudes of little
creatures which I could not distinguish from snow
fleas. If they are not the same they must be
next of kin to the jolly little winter bristletails.
The voyage back toward the sunset was not
eventful. A flock of black ducks passed upstream, flying high and at wonderful speed.
They are far from graceful, but they give one
the impression of immense power of wing. Had
this flock been well harnessed I think they could
have drawn me with them out of sight in golden
haze much faster than would have been comfortable. Redwings sang in every tree top. Crows
took long flights, cawing as they flew. Chickadees in pairs responded to the phœbe note so well
mimicked by my companion. Muskrats swam in
the eddies of the stream. We saw two swimming fast round and round a bunch of maples
standing alone in the water. They paid little

attention to us as we passed. As we reached the Minute-Man the chill of the western snows came upon us more keenly. The coloring of sky, woods and river was exquisite. The mass of the heavens was deep blue. Upon it flakes of cloud rested, taking from the sun the glory of gold and of crimson. Low down in the east a bank of very dark blue clouds made a rich background for the stems of the gleaming birches and the burnished twigs of the willows. Just where the sun sank, gold and orange and crimson mingled to form a gateway through which the day was slowly withdrawing. As we stood under the great elms by the Manse the river repeated the story of the sky. Had Lohengrin floated westward over the gilded water towards that gateway I should have bent my head without surprise to catch those few soul-moving notes by which he says "Farewell."

A BIT OF COLOR.

THURSDAY, April 16, at five o'clock in the afternoon, I reached the shores of Fresh Pond at the point where a branch of the Fitchburg railway crosses the Concord turnpike. This part of Cambridge is soon to be changed in many ways, and is worth a particular description. From the Cambridge Common to the northeast corner of Fresh Pond, Concord Avenue runs almost directly northwest. Beyond this point it bends twenty-five degrees towards the west and continues in that line until it reaches Belmont. In the hollow of this bend, resting on Fresh Pond, lies one of the most picturesque bits of ground in Cambridge. It was formerly the estate of Frederick Tudor, the ice king. A beautiful lawn many acres in extent is fringed with lofty hard‑wood trees, many of which are dying, but all of which are beautiful and worthy of careful preservation and exemption from all but the most necessary trimming. On the water front at the northeastern corner of the pond are two immense ice-houses, now condemned and doomed to early destruc-

tion. Perhaps when they are gone it will be
remembered that they were picturesque. One,
with its buttressed brick walls coated with green
lichens and overhung by a projecting upper story
of gray wood, always reminds me of a gloomy
picture I have seen of an Algerian walled town.
The other, overhanging the pond, raises a tall
gray tower against the sky, and looks down upon
deep water through which broken piles emerge
to cast black shadows in the mist. When these
ice-houses are empty they are sepulchral and
forbidding places to enter. The least sound
awakes echoes in the darkness of the roof. English sparrows flit about and scream, and the air
is heavy with dampness and as cold as a tomb.
On Thursday afternoon I turned in from Concord Avenue toward these ice-houses, following
the freight track, which runs directly towards
them, forming a barrier between Fresh Pond and
a foul swamp which fills, with the Tudor place,
the bend in the avenue. The swamp is a thicket
of willows, button-ball bushes, and birches.
The early willows were in full bloom, their
bright yellow staminate and green pistillate
flowers swaying in the wind. Late willows
were beautiful with their small pink-white
pussies and unfolding leaves crowded on slender
stems. Here and there a tall red maple raised
its branches over the swamp and displayed its

gorgeous flowers in the pale sunlight. The grass, only a few days ago burned over by the frugal but short-sighted city workmen, was brilliantly green, and in places four or five inches long. When July suns beat down upon its roots it may miss its mat of protecting fibres destroyed by fire. A fox sparrow was scratching among the grass roots energetically. Several redwings, song sparrows, and a large flock of English sparrows were at work on the ground near by. From the swamp the music of song sparrows and redwings was incessant.

Passing between the ice-houses and the shanties and hen houses which stand on the opposite side of the track I gained the fringe of lofty trees on the Tudor place. A flicker was guarding her house in a hollow maple. Now, she poked her head out and " flickered " for her mate. Then, he answering not, she came out and drummed furiously on the dead resonant wood by her door post. At last his answer came from a distant tree and she flew away to find him. A female sparrow hawk darted from her nest in the deep hollow of an inaccessible limb, and flew with marvellous grace into the open, wheeled, and dropped upon the outstretched finger of one of the tallest trees of this tall grove. Her mate joined her and perched for a second beside her, while a queer whining chatter came from them. Their coloring is as beautiful as that of the fox sparrow, and if they cannot revive the fainting heart by song, they can give the eye joy by their speed, their perfect grace of flight, and the beauty of their outlines.

On the further side of the neglected lawn nearly a hundred purple grackles were feeding in the grass. They rose, blurring the sky in the north, and darkened the tops of a dozen trees where they perched and " creaked " in disgust at my coming.

Looking across the pond the further shores showed but dimly. A strong east wind had been blowing all day, and the air was heavy with the grayness of the sea. The water was metallic in its lights and shadows, its points of reflected fire and stripes of darkness. Distant banks of birches and willows showed faint tones of green, red, and yellow through the silver veil of the chilly air. Mount Saint Joseph stood up dark and strong in the middle of the opposing shore, its hemlocks and pines yielding black reflections in the sullen water. A train rolled along across Concord Avenue, and stopped at the Fresh Pond station. Its outlines were vague and its smoke seemed part of the gray air, until an open furnace door sent a flood of orange light up through it, and revealed its writhings and alternations of whiteness and blackness as the train puffed on towards the setting sun.

I left the Tudor place and kept on round the pond. First I came to an ugly wound in the high bank, where gravel is being cut away to fill " Black's Nook." Then I passed in order the half-filled Nook, the white ice-houses of the Fresh Pond Ice Company, the great gravel banks on the western side of the pond, the swamp full of blazing red maples, almost as gay in their blossoms as in their ripened foliage last autumn; the "geyser" where Stony Brook water, after its long journey underground from the land of Norumbega, bursts out in clustered jets and falls foaming into Fresh Pond, and finally Mount Saint Joseph itself, none the less picturesque because the white caps of the Sisters are occasionally to be seen flitting back and forth amid its shrubbery. The white caps and their school building are doomed to banishment under the law of eminent domain, and in a few months they, like the ice-palaces of the Tudors, will have been made over to the past.

THE CONQUEST OF PEGAN HILL.

LOOKING southward from the heights above Arlington, Belmont and Waltham, the distant horizon is bounded at one point by a wooded ridge having a bold outline and, to the explorer, a most challengeful air. Contour map and compass declared this ridge to be Pegan Hill, the dominant height of the Needham - Natick region. Taking the 8 o'clock train on the " Woonsocket division," which in my mind had previously been classed with the " Saugus branch " as a railway snare to be avoided, I sought on April 18 the unknown town of Dover. My companion was a determined man who years ago had registered a vow to climb Pegan Hill or perish among its cliffs and forests.

The early morning of April 18 was gray and somewhat chilly. My friend brought an umbrella and overcoat, I wore rubber boots and an overcoat. By noon the mercury had passed 80° and was still vigorous.

As we left the train, maps in hand, Pegan Hill was reported to bear due west. We raised our eyes to meet the challengeful foe. A broad

meadow clad in the tender green of freshly
sprouting grass was encircled by comfortable
farms whose ploughed fields, orchards, elms and
scattered buildings framed it pleasantly. A pair
of brooks wandered across it, met, pledged eternal friendship and passed on united, singing,
looking up blue-eyed towards heaven. High in
the air white-bellied swallows revelled in the
sunlight.   The sweet-breathed west wind bore
to us the kindred songs of the purple finch and
the vesper sparrow, the plaint of the meadow
lark, the drumming of the downy woodpecker
and the cawing of the crow. In a pine grove
near by, the pine-creeping warbler and the chipping sparrow contrasted their monotonous repe-
titions of a single note, the one giving a smooth,
well-rounded trill, the other a sharper, more
pointed one. Beyond the meadow and the farms
lay a sunny pasture hillside, crossed horizontally
by a stone wall, and sparsely marked by pitch-
pines and small savins.   The sky-line of this
gentle slope was curved, drumlin-like.   Westward there was nothing more to see save blue
sky and four cowbuntings flying swiftly across
it.   Where was the tree-crowned rocky summit
we had come to conquer ?   The redwings answered, " Cong-ka-ree, go and see ! "   So we
strolled onward across the meadow, through the
farms and up the slope of the pasture hill.

The air was filled with a silvery haze which made distance mysterious, and the nearer landscape dreamy and full of suggestions of Indian summer. The songs of field sparrows rippled continuously across the hillside. A pigeon woodpecker " flickered " persistently in a grove of maples and chestnuts. While standing behind a stone wall and half concealed by its retinue of bushes we heard a rippling warbler-song and caught a flash of gold and green in a barberry bush close at hand. A slender bird about five inches long, golden olive-brown above and rich yellow beneath, paused in the barberry for us to watch him. As he moved his dainty head we saw that his crown was reddish chestnut, and as he threw up his head to sing we saw that his breast and sides were lightly pencilled with a similar shade. Although I had heard the pine warbler sing, this, a yellow red-poll warbler, was the first of the great migrating family of *Sylvicolidæ* which I had met this spring. As my heart grew warm towards him a crow and a dashing little falcon rose from behind the hill and whirled together in the air. . We promptly forgot the tiny warbler, dropped behind the wall, and fixed our glasses on the falcon, which had alighted on the highest plume of a low pitch-pine. Suddenly it swooped to the ground, caught an insect from the grass, and came to a treetop nearer us. As it alternately caught grasshoppers and perched to eat them and watch for more, we crept from bush to bush nearer to the circle of its hunting-ground. Several times it came within gunshot, and as we saw it from all points of view, its rich coloring was clearly revealed. The top of its head and its tail were brilliant chestnut. Its back was cinnamon, its breast light and finely barred on the sides. Around its throat it seemed to wear a collar formed of alternate bars of black and white. Its head was small, its whole bearing alert, graceful, supple. After watching it for some time we perceived that its mate was hunting in much the same manner part way down the slope of the hill. The birds were sparrow hawks in the perfection of spring plumage.

One of their perches was a rude tripod made of joist. This marked the summit of the hill which we had reached almost without knowing it. Seated at its foot we looked north, east, south and west over the fair meadows, fields and groves of the Charles River valley. The meandering river itself was in sight in every quarter but the southeast, and there its tributaries formed an interlacing barrier. But where was Pegan Hill? We consulted the map.

Due north of us were Lake Waban, Wellesley, and Wellesley College. Across the north and

part of the east the river, its vivid green
meadows, and its ruddy maples led the eye
along. Natick and Sherborn, the one a growing town, the other a tract of farms and pleasant
glimpses of blue water, filled the west. To the
south the view was limited, being cut short
by several rocky ridges of unattractive outlines
and vegetation, which our map said were Clark
Hill and Pine Rock Hill. The centre of all
this country which our eyes delighted to rest
upon, so full was it of beautiful tints, was
marked plainly *Pegan Hill.* A bloodless vic-
tory! We had sought the enemy with mighty
preparations, and behold he had kissed our feet,
and made himself our footstool. The ridge
which had attracted our eyes from Prospect Hill
we felt sure was Pine Rock Hill, equal in height
with Pegan, but covered with a sparse growth
of small deciduous trees promising neither birds,
flowers, nor other inducements for a climb.

At the foot of the hill on the northern side we
found some charming spots on the borders of the
Charles. One was on the Needham side of the
river, where an extensive grove of stately old-
growth white pines overhung a sharp bend in the
stream, making its deep and swift current very
dark in contrast to a flat bit of meadow opposite,
which was radiant with tender green of newly
sprouted grass. A grouse rose from a cool brook

hollow near this bend. A pewee called to us as she hurried through the grove. A flock of five white-bellied swallows cut swift circles against the kindly sky. The voice of the west wind in the ancient pines sang a song full of rest and contentment, and for us, as for the river, it was pleasant and purifying to linger there before going on to the friction and the pollution of the city. In all that day's wandering I saw no sign of terror in any living thing that was not caused by man. Nature by herself is not all peace, by any means, but she is far nearer to it than when man is present.

On the edge of these beautiful pines, as at several other points in our walk, my friend and I were angered to find the largest and finest trees selected as posting places for advertisements ; cloth, paper, wood, and metal signs telling of the supposed merits of certain Boston firms and daily newspapers, having been nailed to the trees. It is hard to say which fact is most disagreeable to contemplate, the boldness of the advertisers in disfiguring private property, or the indifference of the public to the damage done.

Following up the Charles through the pines we reached the Sudbury River aqueduct, and from the top of its sodded embankment gained a near view of Wellesley and its castles of

learning. Looking across the meadows of
Dewing Brook, never greener than at that
moment, we were charmed by the distant picture of feeding cattle, boys fishing in the brook,
snug and well-fashioned farm buildings, lofty
shade trees in full bloom, and behind them the
clustered buildings of the college and the town.
It might have been a mellow fragment of old
England but for the bunch of very new, dirty,
and disorderly shanties which appeared in one
corner of the picture to remind us that New
England is also New Ireland. Entering the
town, we made our way to the railway station
with speed and directness. As it was Saturday
afternoon a fair share of the eight hundred
students (or a share of the eight hundred fair
students) were in the streets, walking, driving,
bicycling, catching trains for town, exercising
dogs, and otherwise disporting themselves. My
companion being a bachelor, still in moderate
years, I sighed with relief when our train started
and I had him safely penned in a front seat
next the window.

THE maple swamps of Alewife Brook are places rich in birds, but they are even richer in foul odors. They are not pleasant at any hour, least of all at sunrise. In order to go from Cambridge in the early morning into any other woods than these, it is necessary to walk quite a long distance, or else to take the first train which goes out from Boston over the Fitchburg tracks. On April 20 I caught this train at Hill's Crossing at 6.41 A. M., having walked out Concord Avenue to the Tudor place, round the northern edge of Fresh Pond, past the slaughter-house opposite Black's Nook and over the mead-ows to the little station. The walk was charm-ing, for at that early hour there were more birds than men in Cambridge streets, and the men were laborers, with earnest faces, strong arms, and brown hands, who seemed close to the soil and its secrets. In the Harvard Observatory grounds a ruby-crowned kinglet was singing. Less than an inch longer than a humming bird, this little creature has one of the most delightful songs known to New England woods. It is very kind of it to sing here when its breeding ground may be two or three hundred miles north of us.

The Fresh Pond trees and fields were alive with birds. Two pairs of flickers were " flickering ; " robins ran on the ground, shouted in the apple-trees, chased each other through the air ; meadow starlings, redwings, and purple grackles could be heard and seen in all parts of the Tudor place. White - bellied swallows danced across the sky, and the harsh rattle of the kingfisher marked the flight of that vigorous bird over the waters of the pond. The dry note of the chipping sparrow was incessant and wearisome, but when the sparrow hawks left their favorite corner and flew with their matchless grace through the grove and across the field, chipping sparrows were forgotten.

I reached Waverley Oaks as the village clock struck seven. In the meadow between Beaver Brook and the railway embankment quantities of watercress were growing, horsetails stood four inches high, and a jolly dandelion turned its round face to the sun. Horsechestnut leaves were open on the 19th, and here in the meadow the ferns were setting free their coils, and leaves on many of the early shrubs were open. Was the bloodroot in bloom? that was the question of the morning. Along the wall between Beaver Brook and the Oaks white buds were pointing heavenward by hundreds. In a spot where the sunlight fell the flowers were opening, and as the warmth of the rays grew stronger, half the glorious company opened their bright eyes to the lovely spring morning. There are few flowers with more purity in their faces than bloodroot. They are made to admire and love growing, not picked. If torn from their roots their dark blood stains the picker's hand, and soils the fair petals of the flowers themselves; even if tenderly borne to a vase they quickly drop their petals, as though mourning their home under the shadow of the barberry bushes.

Seated among these delicate children of the soil, my back against an elm trunk and my figure obscured by the drooping branches of a bush, I watched the birds among the oaks, and near the small pond at the foot of the kame on which some of the oaks grow. The voices of robins, song and chipping sparrows, cow birds, redwings, flickers, and bluebirds filled the air. At first it seemed as though from this chorus single notes could not be detached, but soon the rattle of a kingfisher sounded from on high. Looking up I saw three of these birds flying over towards Waltham and the Charles. They were at a great height for them, and I could not recall ever before having seen more than two flying together. Before they were out of sight a sparrow hawk glided over, and presently a flock of ten or fifteen cedar birds shot past through the trees as though bound for the Mississippi. The oaks seemed to be a good point of observation even if the interesting strangers did not alight. A rushing and rustling of wings, and a queer quacking call marked the swift passage of a duck. Instead of going by, this visitor dropped into the reedy pool in front of me. I could see a part of the pond, the rest was screened by button - ball bushes. Long minutes passed. Should I move, creep up to the pond, or around the kame to its further slope? Something moved on the water beyond the bushes. A dark form — two dark forms — were winding in and out among the stems and coming towards me.

I raised my glass to my eyes and kept it there without a motion during what followed. Two ducks, one following the other, were coming slowly through the bushes which grew in the water at the end of the pond. From the bushes a thread of water wound in and out among the grass tussocks and passed under the wall within twenty short paces of me. The ducks entered this little brook ; the sunlight fell directly upon them. They were wood ducks, the most gorgeous of our waterfowl. Every feather shone

in the strong light. As they came on down
the stream towards me they saw me ; their bright
eyes were fixed upon me. If I moved ever so
little they would be off. I felt frozen, hypno-
tized, by their steady stare. The female was
handsome enough, but the drake was equal to a
Hindu maharajah in his splendor. His breast
was chestnut, his head lustrous green and violet,
his throat white, his back coppery black and
brown with purple and green lights playing over
it, his glittering eye was red. All these colors,
gleaming in the sunlight at once, without so much
as a spear of grass to hide them, were dazzling.
The birds did not seem real. I longed to call
some one to see them, to enjoy them with me.
They slid noiselessly through their narrow channel to the wall, and there the bushes hid them.
Two or three minutes passed ; there was no sign,
no sound. I rose and scanned the meadow for
them, but they had vanished ; and during the
remainder of my hour they did not reappear.
Twice afterwards on other days I saw them, but
under no such favoring circumstances.

From the Oaks I walked most of the way back
to Cambridge, seeing and hearing great numbers
of birds. Bluebirds were conspicuously common ; several more kingfishers flew over ; flickers
were so numerous that I felt sure they must be
migrating in force. Near Payson Park another

sparrow hawk sailed by me. There are known to be four pairs of these beautiful birds breeding within a few miles of Cambridge this spring. If the men hired by the Boston taxidermists to slaughter birds to keep them supplied with attractive material for " the trade " do not kill these exquisite little falcons, the species may soon become comparatively common in eastern Massachusetts. It is one of the most useful and friendly to man of our songless birds.

Not far from Payson Park in Belmont, and to the northwest of Fresh Pond, is what is sometimes called Summer House Hill. I reached this little eminence, which is one hundred and twenty feet above tide water, at about nine o'clock, and gained from it one of those pleasing half far-away, half near-by views which only small hills can give. The near-by was a mingling of orchards alive with birds and carpeted with new grass already several inches long; the Concord turnpike and the brickyards and marshes beyond it; Fresh Pond with its graceful curving shore, drives, groves, and odd old ice-houses; Mt. Auburn, the sky-roofed Westminster of New England; Payson Park with its grand old trees and broad lawns; and Belmont, the picturesque town of terraces and hillside villas. The far-away was Arlington and its wooded heights; Winchester with its church spires; Medford and the Fells flanking the great Boston basin on its north; and the basin itself crowded with the tangled streets and bristling chimneys of half a dozen sister cities. The view on that morning was interesting for a special reason; it presented a sudden change in the coloring of the whole face of the land. A few days earlier, grays, browns, and delicate yellows had prevailed. These were forgotten, swept away by a flood of green and crimson. The green of the meadows, roadsides, and upland hayfields was so vivid that all under-lying tints were obliterated. The willows, which for weeks had been the most conspicuous color-spots in every view, had developed leaves strong enough in color to cancel the golden and coppery tones of their stems and merge them in the greens of grassland and meadow. The maples from gray and mist-like softness had with their red blossoms come forward as the most pro-nounced color-masses in the landscape. Around Fresh Pond and in the maple swamps of the Alewife Brook marshes this gorgeous crimson coloring made the maples as conspicuous as in autumn. The first few days in April the greater part of Massachusetts was white with snow. Such coloring as this, coming as a quick contrast to winter tints, appeals most earnestly to the eye, and leaves a deep impression on the memory. It is one of the potent elements of spring, and serves to attract and impress minds which might, without it, being blind to the subtler beauties and wonders of the transformation, miss altogether the glory of Nature's maidenhood.

A VOYAGE TO HEARD'S ISLAND.

THE Old Manse was sound asleep. The ringing of bells in Concord town, the rippling laughter of a purple finch in the apple-tree, the sharp
" chebec" of a least flycatcher by the barn, even
the noise we made in taking our canoes and
small traps off the express wagon, and carrying
them down through the orchard to the river,
failed to wake the old house from its slumbers.
Song sparrows sang in the vista of lilacs at the
western door, robins ran back and forth on the
lawn like mechanical toys on a nursery floor,
and redwing blackbirds and their naughty, im-
provident cousins the cow buntings creaked,
squeaked, and whistled on the willows by the
Minute-Man. He, at least, was awake. His eager,
resolute face was watching down that eastern path-
way for the coming of new perils or new bless-
ings to the children of Freedom. We left the
Manse to its slumbers and the statue to its eternal vigil, and pushed our frail canoes out upon the
glittering surface of the stream. It was five
o'clock in the afternoon of Friday, April 24th.

A gentle west wind swung the catkins on the poplars, rippled the soft, short grass on the lawn, caressed the new leaves of the horse-chestnuts, maples, and willows, which were timidly unfolding under the unusually encouraging season. The Musketaquid had fallen more than a foot since our last cruise, and it was still falling fast. A greater change had, however, crept over the land and the air. The land was now a garden full of beauty. There was the beauty of miles of velvety grass and sprouting grain; there was the beauty of shrubs thickly clad in half-unfolded leaves; and there was the beauty of tall trees, whose foliage seemed to be growing as the eye rested upon it, and whose outlines of limb and trunk were being disguised by gauzy draperies of green, sure to become denser and fuller day by day as the eager sun looked more ardently upon the earth. There was also the beauty of spring blossoms, the red of the maples, the white of the willows; the yellow of dandelions, early buttercups, and potentilla; the white of saxifrage, everlasting, houstonia, and anemone.

The change in the air was twofold. On our other voyage it had brought the chill of snow from the central parts of the state; now it brought the comforting warmth of a summer-like day. Before, the song of a bird or of a flock of birds had been an item by itself; now, the air was as full of musical undulations as it was of heat waves and light waves. An effort was required, not so much to hear a particular song, as to separate it from the sound ripples which broke unceasingly upon the ear. In the midst of the splendor of the sunset colors, gold and red upon the sky, gold and red upon the river, we urged our dainty craft against the current, bound for Fairhaven Bay.

My canoe was a Rob Roy, my friend's a longer, more slender one, without a deck. As we paddled, we faced forward, and each regulated his course by a lever, which he pressed with his feet, and which was connected with the rudder by chains running under the gunwales of the canoe. Thanks to this device, which is my friend's, we were enabled to use light, single-bladed paddles and to give little thought to the method of our strokes.

It is pleasant to look forward rather than backward as one travels on a river. There is more of hope in it, and consequently more of joy. In rowing, one sees only departing, waning beauty; in paddling, the whole world is before, with its good and evil inviting choice, its promises of wonders beyond distant shores, its ever enlarging beauties, its swiftly realized dreams.

As our paddles rose and fell, scattering bright globules of water on the river, which at first refused to receive them back into itself, we left Concord behind us on the one side, and on the other many a meadow and sloping hillside, crowned with farmhouse or summer cottage. The town did not let us abandon it suddenly. More than once, when I thought it left far away across a meadow, the river would sweep back to it, and show us more green lawns and terraces, gay boats lying on the grass, elms fruited with purple grackles and cowbirds, children at their games, purple martins soaring near their bird boxes, and wagons rolling up dust in the roads. Before we were free from the town our river changed its name ; for at a place where a ledge crowned with great trees is washed by the current, the north branch blends its waters with the Sudbury to form the Concord. The Sudbury was our stream, and but for one brief glance up the dark Assabet I should not have known that Musketaquid had lost a part of its strength.

About seven o'clock our cockleshells came to a long reach of river looking a little east of south. Meadow-grasses rustled over many acres on each side of us, and the breeze favored us at last. So we raised our tiny masts and spread our white sails. That which followed was to physical action what falling asleep is to mental effort. It was not rude motion gained by thumping oars against resisting water. It was more like becoming a part of the air and gliding on in its embrace, silently, swiftly, without friction. Side by side our boats slipped on past whispering grasses, over the black water, under the violet sky in which the high stars were now appearing. Behind us the dark water was broken into ripples. They held quivering, bending bits of color, deep red, orange, yellow, and silver, scattered over the inky blackness of the stream. In front of us was a hill. It seemed very high in the gathering gloom. Nearer and on our right was a grove of lofty white pines. There are few such trees in this part of New England; they are a fragment of the primeval woods, full of wind voices and memories of a lost race of men, and a vanishing race of birds and mammals. As we neared this grove a mysterious greeting came to us from its depths. A voice at once sad, deep, soft, and full of suppressed power seemed to question us. My friend responded in the stranger's language, and a few moments after a dark form floated over us, its great wings making no sound as they beat against the night air. Then from the foot of Fairhaven Hill the voice called to us again; and soon the form passed back over the river to the tops of the pines. Behind Fairhaven Hill the eastern clouds reflected a slowly increasing flood of yellow light. Over the rest of the sky night had settled. Bird voices were hushed, but from the river banks, as far as the ear could hear, the song of frogs rose and fell in irregular rhythm. The air was chilly, and a thin layer of white mist hurried over the surface of the water. Southward, up the river between Fairhaven Hill and the pine woods, the water gleamed with silvery whiteness, reflecting the sky. Its surface narrowed in the distance between looming, wooded headlands, and was finally swallowed up in the shadow of great trees whose tops made a serrated border to the brightening sky. At last the moon's rim showed through the trees on Fairhaven Hill, and the high pines close by us on the western shore were bathed in uncertain light. From their tops the mysterious voice still questioned us at intervals.

This pine grove was our chosen camping ground, and the light of the moon enabled us to select a landing place and to draw our canoes ashore. Soon the two boats were resting upon hollows in the pine needles, ready to serve as our cocoons when we felt the need of sleep ; a bright fire was blazing near the edge of the water at a point where it offered no menace to the safety of the grove, and we were resting our weary muscles and busying our several senses with the moon, cold chicken and marmalade, the warmth of the fire, the aroma of the pines, and the low, shivery remarks of the ghostly owner of the grove. Instead of being alarmed by our landing, the light of our fire, and the sound of our voices, the dark phantom of the pines seemed to be attracted by these unusual interruptions. The voice grew louder and more distinct. Its winged source came nearer from tree top to tree top, until it settled in the tallest, darkest pine in the grove, almost immediately over our heads. It was unlike any other voice I had ever heard. It possessed a contralto quality; it was laden with intense emotion, yet it was calm and singularly regular both in its sounds and in its silences. In spite of its softness and the slight trembling in its tones, it suggested power, — a power sufficient to raise a trumpet note audible a mile away.

Ten o'clock came and went, and we sought our cocoons. Over the opening in my Rob Roy a rubber blanket was arranged to button tightly, leaving space only for my face. Over the entire canoe, supported by a cord run from a short mast aft to the short mast near the bows, was drawn a waterproof tent having two little netting-covered windows in its gable ends. Wrapped in my wool blanket, tightly buttoned under the rubber blanket, I sighed, thought how sleepy I was, how well the canoe sustained my weary limbs, how comfortable I was to be, and — in fact, I was on the eve of sweet slumber when, " Whōō, hoo-hoo-hoo, whōōō, whōōō ! " came from the tree just over me. The voice restored me to consciousness. I seemed to see through my tent and the darkness of the pine foliage to the top of the tree, where in the moonlight sat a great bird with staring yellow eyes and feathery horns, looking now at the moon on her voyage from Fairhaven westward, and then at our smouldering fire, or at *me*, supine in my mummy case. " Whōō, hoo-hoo-hoo, whōōō, whōōō ! " came again, and its melancholy vibrations set my nerves to its rhythm, so that after it ceased it seemed to continue to echo in my mind's ear. Wide awake, I found myself measuring the time until it should come again. " Whōō, hoo-hoo-hoo, whōōō, whōōō ! " The thrill which the last two prolonged sighing notes sent through me was wonderful. They seemed to penetrate every fibre of my brain and quiver there as heated air quivers before the eye at midsummer midday. I thought of the theory that birds' notes are but imitations of sounds which they hear most frequently, and this song of the great horned owl above me seemed akin to the moaning of night winds in the hollows of dead trees.

After a sleepless hour or more had passed, I sat up and peered out of the little window at the

head of my coffin. There were the great pine
trunks rising like roughly carved columns to
support the dark roof above. The moon's rays
came between them and fell full in my face. I
could see up the river, whose ripples were full of
bits of moonlight and black shadows, over which
hurried shreds of mist. Quiet as was the night,
nothing seemed asleep. Nature, shamming repose, was moving silently about on mysterious
errands of which slumbering man was not to
know. The moon sailed on with her convoy of
stars westward, the clouds sailed eastward. The
river flowed northward, the mists were moving
southward. Thousands of frogs mingled their
songs on the river banks. The woods were full
of slight rustlings of leaves, creakings or snap-
pings of twigs, squeaks which seemed vocal, and
an undercurrent of sound which was like the
hushed breathing of the earth. Then, as though
guiding all, came the weird voice of the owl in
its strange rhythm and its stranger intonation.

  Midnight passed and went on its long way,
but still I did not sleep. Each time the owl
spoke I was listening for it. Then a drumming
partridge and the frogs gained a share of my
hearing and thinking. The latter were leopard
frogs, and their chorus was pitched on a low
key. One of my friends compares their music
to an army snoring in unison; another to a

giant gritting his teeth. I could make my ears assent to either comparison. Suddenly my vibrating nerves told me that the song of the owl had changed. I listened, excited. " Whōō, hoo-hoo-hoo, whōōō, whōōō!" No, it was the same. But hark! from another tree comes back a response, " Whōō, hoo-hoo-hoo, hoo-hoo-hoo, whōōō!" The male had returned from a hunting trip, and the pair were talking it over.

Whether it was the change and alternation in the owl's metre, or simple exhaustion on my part, which at last gave me sleep I cannot say, but after hearing a distant deep-toned bell strike twice I lost myself in needed slumber.

My awakening was sudden. I found myself leaning on my elbow listening to one of the most joyous songs which New England birds produce. " Cherokee, cherokee, bo-peep, bo-peep, chrit, chrit, chrit, perucru, perucru, cru, cru, cru, cru!"

Pushing aside tent and mummy cloths I unsnarled myself and gained my feet. The moon was nearing her western harbor, but upon the rim of Fairhaven Hill rested the morning star. There are few moments in life so full of happiness and exultation as those in which man, brushing sleep from his eyes, rises with the first bird song and welcomes into his soul the beauty of the dawn. Some minutes in a life seem doubly charged with the essence both of self-consciousness and of perception. That moment of awakening was one of them to me. In this world or the next I shall ever be able to recall the clarion of that brown thrush, the pure beauty of that star, and the contour of hill and forest, river and tented boats. I aroused my friend, and we sought a high, open pasture behind the pines, where we noted the order in which bird songs or calls reached us. The song sparrow, the whip-poor-will, the robin, the crow, the chickadee, the ruby-crowned kinglet, the field sparrow, came in quick succession, the last reaching us at twenty minutes past four. The partridge had drummed all night. If the owls had been silent at all it was for little more than an hour.

Not long after the sun swung clear of Fairhaven Hill our voyage upstream was resumed. The wind came from a bank of cold gray clouds, which rose rapidly from the north and soon obscured sun, moon, and pale blue sky. A spring flowing from a rugged ledge filled our jug with ice-cold water. On the ledge, columbine was in full bloom, a fact not often recorded for the 25th of April. Beyond, lay Fairhaven Bay, a beautiful widening of the river framed in wooded hills. Upon the crest of one of these hills stood three pines, and into the middle one a hawk descended upon its nest. Beyond the bay came a belt of meadow shore where the wind had a wide sweep.

Here we came upon a wounded sheldrake, whose quick and clever diving and desperate beatings along the tops of the waves enabled him to escape us. In the river's wandering across this meadow it led us close to a charming home spot. A high hill, broken on the river side into many gray ledges, overhung a narrow, bright green field. This was the home acre. A house surrounded by shrubbery, a barn blessed with calves, hens, broods of young chickens, a kitchen garden newly planted, an orchard with swelling flower buds, a bridge with many piers and a bright red boat moored near it, — all these things lay cosily under the ledges. Swallows flew merrily back and forth between meadow and barnyard, and a bluebird sang sweet music in an apple-tree. We paused under the bridge and took account of the weather. The wind was rough and came in gusts ; the sky was now completely overcast, and in the north ugly clouds seemed pressing forward up the river. Oilskin coats and rubber covers for the tops of the canoes were brought into play, and then away we sped under reefed sails across the next mile of river. Rain, hail, and snow all pelted us, and helped the wind lash the river into foam.

An hour before noon we landed at a hillside covered with pines and cedars, and sought shelter in the woods for dinner and a fire. The hill

sloped towards the south and commanded a view
of a wide bend in the river, and beyond it the
beginning of the great Sudbury meadows, now
under water and more like a shallow lake than a
stream. Kept dry by the pines and in a glow by
a fire of dry twigs and pine needles, we watched
the strange mingling of seasons before us. An
angry sky blotched with luminous white and
leaden gray; a river flowing against the storm,
covered with white caps, foam, and the paths of
sudden " flaws ; " beyond, flat grass land and a
birch wood forming a background for the swaying columns of snowflakes, which were whirled up
the stream, across the drenched fields and out of
sight over the meadows, — such was the wintry
side of the picture. Nearer, was a grassy slope
of the tenderest green flecked with everlasting,
saxifrage, anemones, small purple violets of at
least two kinds, white violets, innocents, as I love
to call houstonia, early buttercups, potentilla, and
dandelions. In the pines or within earshot were
robins, hermit thrushes, pine warblers, a parula
warbler, chipping sparrows, song sparrows, and
field sparrows. Such was the spring-like side of
the picture. Squall after squall passed, but the
warblers sang on, and the swallows skimmed the
river and seemed as gay among snowflakes as
among sunbeams.

As the water on the Sudbury meadows was so

shallow that more was to be feared from grounding than from tipping over, we hoisted sail and let the storm winds do their wildest with us. The canoes careened, the sheets tugged until our hands ached holding them, and off we flew like parts of the driving scud, up the long miles of meadow. Here and there bushes, or tussocks of swamp grass, reared their heads above the water and warned us from the shallows, but in the main the course was clear, and we passed over it as swiftly as the storm itself.

About three o'clock the sun came out, and we found ourselves near Wayland village. Sheltered from the wind by a railway embankment, we clung to the edge of a half-submerged meadow, to watch the flight of swallows after the storm. Perhaps we saw a thousand swallows that day, or perhaps my friend's usually conservative mind was too excited to estimate fairly. There were enough at all events to cover every rod of meadow with the poetry of geometry, drawn again and again in living lines of lustrous blue and black, warm chestnut, and gleaming white. The white-bellied swallows outnumbered all others ten to one, but in the maze could be seen barn swallows, bank swallows, eaves swallows, and now and then a purple martin or a chimney swift. Away to the west was Nobscot Hill. Eastward, not more than a mile

distant, was Wayland village, and just ahead
was the sunny slope of Heard's Island, our *ulti-
ma Thule.* Nothing short of another snow-squall
could have made us leave the dancing swallows,
but the squall came, and we sought Heard's Island and friendly firesides.

After resting a bit we put on all the warm
clothes we could muster, and took a brisk walk
to Heard's pond, which bounds the island on the
southwest, and to the Wayland elm, the noblest
tree in Massachusetts. The cold appealed to us
as strongly as though February had come again,
and we feared that the birds, buds, and flowers
would suffer during the night. Heard's pond
is a charming sheet of water, soon doubtless to
become the centre of a circle of cheery summer
cottages. As for the Wayland elm, it is a wonderful triumph of nature. As we paced under
it from north to south, its ancient branches
seemed to extend over one hundred and twenty-
five feet from one side of its lawn to the other.
Two very large elms which stand near it are
dwarfed by its royal size. Its symmetry, the perfect condition of its many branches and myriad
twigs, the healthy state of its unscarred bark,
and the simple dignity of its position, all make it
an ideal tree, — one which a savage might adore
as the abiding place of a spirit. That night the
canoes slept alone on the edge of the cold mead-

ow, and my slumbers were presided over, not by
great horned owls, but by time-honored pictures
of Dante, Petrarch, Tasso, Louis Agassiz, and
Benjamin Peirce, and of Rome, Tivoli, Venice,
Florence, and fair Harvard.

Sunday dawned cool, clear and windy. There
had been no frost. Nature had been true to
herself, as she generally is. From nine till six
we fought our way homewards against impetuous
winds. No sail could aid us, no current do more
than mitigate the force of the air. The battle
against the waves developed a marked difference
in our canoes. The moment we rounded a curve
into a stretch of wind-swept water my canoe
shot ahead of the other without extra effort on
my part. In still water, and especially towards
evening, when the wind died out, my friend was
the one who played with his paddle, and I the
one who toiled. At two o'clock we landed at
the foot of a bold ledge rising abruptly sixty or
seventy feet from the stream. We climbed part
way to the summit and lunched, surrounded by
columbine, violets, saxifrage and dozens of birds.
A pewee complained of us, and turning we saw
her nest on the face of the ledge, hidden under a
projecting shoulder of rock. It was just completed, and its delicate moss trimming made it
seem part of the lichen-grown ledge itself. From
the pines came the thin voice of a black-throated

green warbler saying, " one, two, three-a, four,"
and not far away the strong, brave phrases of
the solitary vireo were audible. A real treat
was the song of the ruby-crowned kinglet. It
reminds me of a favorite mountain cascade of
mine deep in hemlock woods, which has sparkling jets, quick twists in its descending current,
unbroken rushes over polished rock, and then
three or four plunges, ending in a dark pool
where trout linger under the foam. As we
looked over the water a pair of wood ducks flew
by, and at another time a small flock of black
ducks. A kingfisher passed and repassed, sound-
ing his harsh rattle, and a great blue-gray and
white marsh hawk sailed down stream along the
meadow.

We camped that night eighteen miles from
Heard's Island and three miles below the Minute-Man. Ball's Hill rose above us, and Great
Meadow, now half above water, extended before
us like a wide lagoon. The curving shore was
thickly strewn with pieces of dry wood of curi-
ous shapes. When my friend stated that there
was a wooden pail factory on the Assabet I un-
derstood the origin of our fuel supply. During
the last mile of the voyage, and while we were eating our supper, we heard a bittern " pumping "
on the meadow. At sunrise next morning two
could be heard from the top of the hill, one

up stream and another down towards Carlisle bridge. The syllables " pung-chuck " repeated three or four times give an idea of this sound when it is made at a distance. After dark, as we lingered by our fire, we heard the " quauk " of a night heron flying down stream. I slept as well that night in my narrow mummy case as I should have on my broad spring bed at home.

To see a sunrise from the top of Ball's Hill on a warm still day in April is worth an eighteen-mile paddle. There were bitterns pumping, crows cawing, mourning doves cooing, grouse and woodpeckers drumming, blackbirds creaking, kingfishers rattling, and a throng of thrushes, warblers, and finches singing in that early mass at St. Ann's. The sun came up behind Bedford towers, cast golden rays upon Great Meadow and passed into gray clouds. Although we expected rain we spent half the forenoon coasting along Carlisle shore and wandering through the pine woods. I found a snug little screech owl in a hole in an apple-tree and tried to induce him to come out. No pounding on the tree nor gentle poking of him produced any effect. He was as placid as though made of the dead leaves and decayed wood which his coloring most suggested. A towhee bunting and his mate were scratching in the dry leaves by the river side. They, like the fox sparrows, seem to work both feet at once in scratching. It was a proud sight

when a high-flying osprey plunged downward
through many a foot of air to the river, and scattered myriad drops as he struck the water in a
vain effort to grasp a wary fish. A pair of red-
shouldered hawks screamed angrily at us as we
paddled past their chosen grove. A bittern flew
up stream and settled in a snarl of rushes. We
marked the spot and my friend paddled to it.
The bird allowed the bow of the canoe to come
within six or seven feet of him before his confi-
dence in his protective coloring failed sufficiently
to make him fly. A spotted sandpiper flew from
shore to shore ahead of us, giving his character-
istic whistle as he sped low over the water.
When he remained for a moment on the shore
his " teetering " seemed to make his outlines
blend in the river ripples. The water thrush,
a warbler next of kin to the ovenbird, has the
teetering habit to a less marked degree, and is
also a bird whose life is passed near the edge of
waves.

Not long after midday we sighted the Minute-
Man, passed under his wooden bridge and
grounded our boats on the Old Manse shore. A
happy voyage was over. We had met fifty-seven
kinds of birds and seen eighteen or more kinds
of flowers in bloom. We had killed nothing,
not even time, for those sixty-seven hours will
live as long as our memory of pleasant things
serves us.

A FOREST ANTHEM.

THE 30th of April was a hot day. I left Boston at 12.30 P. M., in a car marked for the White Mountains via Conway Junction. The country was beautifully green, and some early fruit trees were white with flowers. In the brook meadows the marsh marigolds were gleaming like gold coin, and now and then we passed a pasture whitened by houstonia. As we rolled over the Ipswich and Rowley marshes the dunes showed their ragged ranges against the eastern sky, and the sunlight brought out the beauty of their coloring. I was struck by the indifference to the cars of many of the wild creatures we passed. A woodchuck trundled his fat body slowly over a sandy field and scarcely looked at the train. Crows often walked up and down a stubble field within fifty feet of the track and merely kept one eye on the rushing, dust-raising cars. Near Kittery an eagle drew nearer and nearer to the train as though interested by it. On the other hand, sheep and dozens of awkward spring lambs fled from us, and horses kicked up their heels and galloped away in their pastures, or shied in harness, to the terror of nervous women.   After passing Wolfborough Junction I watched for traces of winter, but Wakefield and Ossipee were as green as Concord and Cambridge.   Marigolds shone by the brooks, arbutus smiled from the shady banks along the cuttings, maples glowed red in the descending rays of the sun.   The leaves on birches and poplars were well out and brilliant in color.   Swallows were skimming over Bearcamp water, and smoke hung over the mountains so that even Chocorua's peak was not in view until I reached West Ossipee and left the train.

Half of the country between the Ossipee Mountains and Chocorua is a sandy level covered with pitch-pines and scrub-oaks.   It is a fine place for blueberries, fires, and pine warblers in summer, for crows, golden rod, and asters in autumn, and for snowdrifts in winter.   Now and then one gets a glimpse of a deer among the scrub, and in winter fox tracks are always thick upon the snow which lies heavy upon these plains.   As the sun sank low in the west the air became chilly and the snow wrinkles on Chocorua's brow seemed more real.   Towards the east a tower of smoke rose into the sky, and at one point I caught a glimpse of the flames not more than a mile away.   By seven I was supping at a cosy fireside in Tamworth Iron

Works village, listening to tales of winter hardships and spring sickness, for the grip had been making hearts weary even in these fastnesses of the north. Then under the light of the stars I walked on up the Chocorua River valley towards the lakes and the mountain, at whose feet my haven nestled. Lights gleamed and were lost in the valley behind me. Dull masses of firelight shone upon the smoky sky in three places on the horizon. A torch flashed, went down, and flashed again, marking a spot where a fisherman was watching, spear in hand, for suckers in a meadow brook. Then, as I reached the crest of the hill, I saw below me the white water of the lakes, and beyond, above, dimly present in the smoky heaven as conscience is present in the mind of man — *Chocorua.*

The stars burned near it like altar candles. The smoke of fires rose around it like incense, the song of myriad frogs floated softly from the lakes below like the distant chanting of a choir, and the whispering of the wind in the pines was like the moving of many lips in prayer.

Early the next morning I was out under the cloudless sky listening to the voices of May day. Sparrows were in the majority. Song, field, chipping, vesper, white-throats, and juncos were all there, the white-throats being the most numerous. White-bellied and barn swallows

circled around the cottage, and chimney-swifts
dotted the sky with their short, sharp notes.
Loons were making wild clamor on the lake, the
phœbe note of the chickadee came like a cool
breeze from the orchard, and up in the sugar-
maple grove a pigeon woodpecker was calling
" flick-flick-flick-flick-flick-flick " a great many
times in succession. The air was superlatively
pure, sparkling, full of that which makes deep
breathing a pleasure. The great mountain
peak stood out sharply against the northern sky,
and the morning sunbeams came back dancing
from its snowdrifts. Peace pervaded everything, yet a thrill of life was trembling in earth
and air and water. Spring, real spring was
present in that land, with no threat of east wind
to chill it. In the woods, beside the roads,
the arbutus grew in masses. Its leaves were
flattened to earth, just as the snow had left
them. To find the blossoms one had to run a
finger down the stems and lift up the shy
flowers to the light of day. Their perfume made
the air precious. The straw-colored bells of the
uvularia swung in the breeze. In the woods
by the brookside the painted and the dark red
trilliums hid their beauty, but in every grove,
upon the sides of the mountains, and along the
shores of the lakes, the blossoms of the maples
glowed red in the sunlight.

All through the day the white-throated sparrows scratched in the leaves which the melting snows had left pressed to the surface of the ground. I estimated that I saw over a hundred of these busy birds. A few were singing, and their " pe-pe-pe-pe-peabody, peabody, peabody " went straight to the heart — just as it always does, whether in spring, summer or autumn. I caught one beautiful male who had flown through an open doorway and was beating himself against the window pane. Holding him gently but firmly in my closed hand, so that his wonderfully marked head alone was free to move, I stroked his black, white, and yellow feathers with the tip of my right forefinger. After repeated pressure of the gentlest kind on the back of his beautiful head and the nape of his neck, I slowly opened my hand and left him perched on my middle finger. He looked around him but did not offer to fly. Again and again I brought my hand up slowly to his head and caressed him. His clear, bright eyes watched me fearlessly. I moved him gently, but the little feet only clung the more closely to my finger. For nearly five minutes he perched there contentedly, and then, recovering some suppressed faculty, he rejoined his friends among the dry leaves.

About noon I visited a red maple which I

knew had been a favorite sap-drinking resort of
the yellow-bellied woodpeckers and their attend-
ant friends, the humming birds. The woodpeckers were at the tree, but unaccompanied as yet
by hummers. There was evidence in the large
number of new holes already cut in the bark of
the tree that the woodpeckers had been back
from the south since about April 20. They
were busy excavating a new house in a sound
poplar tree near their maple fountain, and that
also showed a week or more of thought and labor
expended. Black and white creeping warblers
and Nashville warblers were abundant in the
woods near by, and I suspected a downy woodpecker of having selected a house-lot near the
sapsuckers, from the close watch which he kept
on me while I was in the neighborhood. During the half hour which I spent watching the
yellow-bellied woodpeckers drinking the flowing
sap on the maple and digging diligently at their
hole in the poplar, I heard an unbroken cawing
of crows at a distance. At last the uproar was
so great that I went to seek an explanation of it.
Well hidden on the crest of a kame, I looked
across a narrow ravine into the edge of a hanging wood of old beeches and yellow birches.
Sixteen crows were in these trees, gathered within a few yards of each other. They were all cawing at once, and shaking their heads, flapping

their wings and hopping back and forth from branch to branch. The centre of attraction seemed to be an idea, not carrion or an owl. I tested this by hooting like a barred owl. Instantly sixteen pairs of wings brought sixteen excited birds across the ravine in search of hated Strix, but I lay low under a hemlock and the crows returned to their rendezvous and their clamorous debate. Several times during the afternoon faint echoes of their oratory reached me at my house half a mile away.

At sunset I walked to the rustic bridge between the lakes and let the wonderful beauty of the scene flow in and fill every corner of my being. Against the northern sky rose Chocorua, Paugus, Passaconaway and Whiteface, four connected mountains, each beautiful, but all differing one from another. Chocorua on the east, and due north of the lakes, sustains a horn of naked rock upon shoulders of converging wooded ridges. Paugus, heavily wooded, yet with many ledge faces and scars showing light among its hemlocks, is a mountain of curves and wrinkles, having no one definite summit, but many fire and wind swept domes. Passaconaway is an immense spruce-covered pyramid, pathless and forbidding. Whiteface, at the west, is a shoulder of rock 4,000 feet high, draped in forest except where an avalanche has rent its covering and

left bare its substance.   All of these peaks
rested upon a sky of gold flecked with crimson.
All of them were repeated in the placid lake,
which also copied the glory of the sky and of
the descending sun.   To the east of the lake a
forest of ancient pines extends from the shore
part way up a ridge.   Above the pines the
ridge is covered with young birches, poplars
and maples.   The tender foliage of these trees,
bathed in the last rays of the sun, formed a
glowing veil of color.   The most delicate greens
showed where young leaves were unrolling on
poplars and birches, soft reds covered the maples,
and the silvery white perpendicular lines of the
birch stems formed a thousand graceful columns
for the support of the light masses of color which
clung to them.   That the sky behind this gay
fresco of the spring was pure pale blue only
added to its loveliness.   Lake, mountains, woods,
sky gave joy to the eye and peace to the heart.
Watching them I said: " Had they but a voice,
how eloquent it would be of praise, how full of
courage and hope.   The lake is pure and deep,
the mountains strong and high, the woods hope-
ful and kind, the sky infinite and full of mystery."   Then there came from the midst of the
dark pines nearest the shore a voice, and it
seemed to me that no other voice in all that wild
New Hampshire valley could have come so near

expressing the praise, hope, and beauty of that spot as the song which floated softly out from the shadows. Those who from childhood have known the song of the hermit thrush, and had it woven into the very fibres of their hearts, will know how I was thrilled by the voice of that hermit thrush, singing on May-day evening at the foot of Chocorua, while snow still gleamed on the mountain summits.

Strolling up the road south of the lakes I suddenly heard the nasal call of a woodcock coming from a dry and sloping field facing the sunset. Soon he rose, and the sound, like that of a singing reed, came through the air. I looked up and presently saw the bird circling irregularly in the upper air, his wings beating rapidly. Jumping the wall I hurried to the spot from which he had risen. No sooner had I crouched among the bushes than the water-whistle notes came nearer and nearer, and then there was a great rushing of swift wings and the bird alit within a few paces of me. He immediately began making a soft and odd note as a substitute for his "'n-yah!" I had heard it described by the syllables "puttle," but as it reached me, it lacked the definiteness and disjunctive quality of those sounds. That the bird saw me I did not doubt for a moment. He faced me, and in the dim light I seemed to feel his close set eyes fixed upon me. I could not see that he moved head or wings in making his inquiring note. After a shorter rest than usual he rose westward in a long diagonal over the bushes and began his circling. The next time he came down he was a hundred feet distant, and began at once the nasal call. In all he made ten or eleven ascents, and in coming down avoided me, although I changed my ground each time he rose and tried hard to get near him again. He finally moved to another field, where he was circling at half past seven, when I left the hill.

Early next morning when I returned to the city my eyes were full of visions of beautiful mountain scenery, and my ears rang with the mocking laughter of loons and the sweet song of the hermit thrush.

THE BITTERN'S LOVE SONG.

On Saturday, May 9, spring had the sulks. In the afternoon a bitterly cold east wind depressed birds, discouraged flowers, turned the sky gray, and left the sun looking like a red wafer. So dim was it that at four o'clock I turned my opera glass on it and scanned it as though it were only the moon. If a May east wind has this chilling effect upon the sun, what wonder that its blast makes poor mortals miserable!

The sun had a black spot on his face. It looked large enough to be Mercury or Venus taking a transit on the sly.

I went by an afternoon train to Waverley and walked thence to Rock Meadow on Beaver Brook. Maps of recent date call this brook "Clematis Brook," a pretty name, no doubt, but one never approved by the General Court. It was at the foot of Rock Meadow that the beavers made their dam, lived, died, and passed into history. Surely the branch of the brook where the beavers lived should be called Beaver Brook, rather than the branch where beavers never lived and never could have lived, owing to the lack of a good place for their dam. Moreover, the "Clematis Brook" of the railway guide and the real estate office is the Beaver Brook sung of by a writer whose knowledge of Cambridge and its surroundings has never been challenged. Here is his description of the old mill which once stood at the cascade just above the Waverley oaks : —

> Climbing the loose-piled wall that hems
> The road along the mill pond's brink,
> From 'neath the arching barberry stems,
> My footstep scares the shy chewink.

> Beneath the bony buttonwood
> The mill's red door lets forth the din ;
> The whitened miller, dust-imbued,
> Flits past the square of dark within.

> No mountain torrent's strength is here ;
> Sweet Beaver, child of forest still,
> Heaps its small pitcher to the ear
> And gently waits the miller's will.

In a note written June 16, 1891, Mr. Lowell says : "You are right. The brook which was down by the great oaks was certainly called ' Beaver ' when I first knew it more than fifty years ago. The scene of my poem was the little millpond, somewhat higher up towards the north, below which was a waterfall in whose company I often passed the day."

The old mill and its miller have long since

been swept away by the currents of Beaver Brook and of that greater stream called Life. The millstone lies below the dam, with moss, not flour, on its cheek. Clematis twines itself over the ruin and seeks even to twine its name over the name hallowed by time and song.

The willows along Concord turnpike where that venerable causeway crosses Rock Meadow are wonderful places for birds. Even on this bleak, discouraged afternoon I saw over thirty species, including eight kinds of warblers. One of them was the black-throated blue warbler, dark, dignified and exclusive. Above he is slaty-blue; below, white. His throat, chin and face are jet black. On each wing he carries a triangular white spot, which marks him as far as the eye can distinguish his dainty form. His wife dresses in green and is one of the "wonder birds" to young collectors, but she may be identified by the white spot on her wing. Another warbler met for the first time this season was the chestnut-sided. His head is yellow on top, his back is dark, his under parts white. His eye is in a black patch, and running from it down his side is a chestnut streak, or series of streaks, often very distinct. I once found a nest of a chestnut-sided warbler, in which young birds were nearly ready to fly, placed in the crotch of a brake, and having no other support. The brakes grew thickly over more than an acre of sparse woodland, and this nest bore the same relation to the miniature forest that an osprey's ponderous structure does to stunted woods by the seashore.

Another bird which I was pleased to see was the kingbird. Three chilly individuals of this pugnacious species sat close together on a willow limb, now and then one of them flying up with a harsh chatter to catch an insect on the wing. While watching these kingbirds I fancied that I heard the sound of a bittern "pumping." It was just six o'clock, and the sound seemed far away, but I scanned the meadow carefully through a gap in the willows. About a hundred yards from the road was a pile of weathered meadow hay, containing perhaps two or three pitchforks-full. On this stood a bittern. His coloring harmonized with it so well that at first I mistook him for a bundle of it poked up against a stake. I watched him for nearly ten minutes, part of the time from the road, later from behind a bunch of bushes fifty feet nearer to him. Four times during this period he made his singular call. His body seemed to be carried about at the angle of a turkey's. His neck was much curved. Suddenly the lower part of the curve was agitated in a way to suggest retching, and a hint of the sound to come later became faintly audible. Then the agitation, which became much more violent, affected the upper throat, neck and head, the head being thrown violently upward and the white upon the throat showing like a flash of light every time the spasmodic fling of the neck was repeated. The sound at that short distance was different in quality from the bittern's note carried to a distance. I fancied that it suggested the choking and gurgling of a bottle from which liquid is being poured, the bottle during the process being held inside an empty hogshead. In trying to approach the bird more closely I alarmed him, and he slunk off into the high meadow grass beyond the haycock. At a distance the sound seemed like two words, " pung chuck," but near by there seemed to be a third syllable ; and several minor sounds, inaudible at a distance, were made while the bird was getting up steam. It seemed to me at the time, knowing nothing of the nature of the process, that the bird produced the sound by a mechanical use of a column of air extending from its open mouth to its stomach. Perhaps whooping cough is perennial in the bittern family.

In this meadow the marsh marigolds were abundant, but on seeking to gather a bunch I felt the first sorrow of the year. The flowers were faded, their golden petals were stained and

partly fallen, their beauty had departed.   So
soon!   Spring, scarcely sure of its standing
as a season, is marked with the first scars of
death.   Not far away I saw a dandelion gone to
seed.   Truly if the winter is tempered by many
a suggestion of the renewal of life, the spring is
branded with many a reminder of the coming of
death.   Life and death; what are they but the
swinging of a pendulum, — the one as sure to
succeed the other as the other is certain to give
place to the one.   Each, while it lasts, contains
an ever increasing germ of the other.   Neither
can be final so long as law exists.

I FULLY intended to climb Nobscot Hill on Sunday, May 10th, but when I reached the Massachusetts Central Railway Station in North Cambridge, I found that there were no Sunday trains, my apparently straightforward time-table to the contrary notwithstanding. Blessing that railway, as I had frequently blessed it before, I hurried back to Porter's Station and took a train on the Fitchburg. Just where I was to leave that train I was uncertain. It was my hope that the conductor, or the brakeman, could tell me which station was nearest to Nobscot Hill. So I went to South Acton and changed to a train for Marlborough. Neither conductor nor brakeman had ever heard of Nobscot Hill, and said there were so many hills I could get out almost anywhere and find what I wanted. As no impressive hill could be seen from the car windows, I finally left the train at a place called Rockbottom. A merciless red sun beat down upon the little village. Scarcely a breath of air was stirring. The loiterers around the station were Irish mill operatives who knew nothing and seemed to care nothing about the natural surroundings of their home. The only one who showed even kindly curiosity felt sure that Honeypot Hill was what I meant, and pointed out a shadeless gravel bubble just across the Assabet. Finding an old resident I learned that Nobscot Hill was six or seven miles away in Sudbury. Could I hire a horse? No, it would be impossible to secure one.

Left to the treeless fields of Rockbottom, the meadows of the listless Assabet and the allurements of Honeypot Hill, I felt something akin to despair gnawing at my temper. I could not even go home, for the next train did not start for the city until six P. M. The heat was worthy of July, but in spite of it I chose the railway embankment as a short cut across the Assabet and its meadows to the only piece of woods in sight. Dressed as warmly as on my January walks, for the wind had been east and the sky cold when I left Cambridge, I strolled down the half-mile of track, enjoying Nature as an Esquimaux might enjoy the Sahara. The sun's light caught in the ripples of the Assabet, and each reflection seemed a flame. An oriole sang from the midst of a snowy pinnacle of pear blossoms, and his plumage seemed to burn in its midst. Two tiny redstarts chased each other in irregular circles above the bushes, and as I glanced at

them fire seemed devouring their expanded tails
and wings. Down in the alders by the riverside a blackbird called out, " Cong-ka-ree —
for I see thee," and then he hovered over the
marsh grass till red - hot spots appeared on
his shoulders. Fortunately for eyes and brain
the pine woods were gained at last, and I
squirmed under a barbed wire fence and took
refuge in their soothing shade.

Lying there I reflected, and my conclusion
was that it was a better day to keep quiet under
the pines by Assabet water than to climb the
slopes of Nobscot Hill. The hot air trembled
with the songs of birds, and wandering songsters
passed under or over the pines, sometimes pausing in their branches. The noisy calls and only
half-musical notes of the robin rang out again
and again. A veery or Wilson's thrush complained of my intrusion. He reminded me that
his cousins, the hermits, had gone north before
this, and were even then singing their hymns
in the cloisters of the hemlock forests. Over the
river a brown thrush was pouring out his rol-
licking song, and in a ditch by the railway track
a catbird sat among briers and flung out alter-
nating bits of music and spiteful complaint.
One bluebird sat on the telegraph wire, and
another on an apple-tree at the foot of Honeypot
Hill. First one and then the other murmured

a comment or a word of love. If it was a comment it was full of happy content; if a word of love it must have sounded very sweet to its mate. Back and forth over the Assabet and its meadows passed the white-bellied swallows. The sunlight found favor in the blue lustre of their backs, and as they rose and fell, turned left or turned right, the immaculate whiteness of their under plumage also responded, flashing to the touch of light. They are my favorites among the swallows. The martins are dark and strong, the bank swallows small and lacking in individuality ; the eaves swallows irregularly distributed and petulant, the barn swallows less graceful in flight and less perfect in form. As for the swifts they are not swallows, and if they were, they seem to be only animated forms of soot possessed of the power of flying through space with incredible speed, and of steering themselves without tails.

The bushes and grasses in and upon the banks of the Assabet were alive with red-wing blackbirds. The males, gay in plumage, noisy and restless, seemed to pervade the meadows. The females, smaller, sober in dress and more chary of speech, flitted back and forth in everlasting bustle. I saw no bobolinks. Occasionally the plaintive call of a meadow starling blended with the blackbird

clamor, and at brief intervals the cheerful dis-
cord of the Baltimore oriole joined the din.
Within the grove there was a lesser circle of
motion and noise. The harsh voice or the
passing shadow of a crow made the warblers in
that inner circle seem more like fractions of
bird life than separate, animated beings. In all,
I count upon seeing nineteen species of warblers
during the migration. It is possible to see
several more kinds, but I refer to my regular
friends. The outrunners of the migrating
horde are the pine warblers, yellow - rumps,
yellow red-polls, black-and-white creepers, summer yellow - birds, and black - throated green
warblers. These are followed by the redstarts,
black - throated blues, parulas, chestnut - sided
warblers, blackburnians, bay - breasteds, Nash-
villes, ovenbirds and accentors, and at varying
times by the Maryland yellow-throats, Wilson's
black-caps, Canadian flycatchers and black-polls,
the last-named sounding the knell of the migration with their irritating z-z-z-ing. This hot day
by the Assabet was evidently just to the liking
of the warblers. Their thin voices sounded in
every direction. A female redstart pursued her
mate round and round and round the grove,
only stopping for a second's rest, in which her
sharp little voice filled the chinks in her circle
of perpetual motion. A succession of yellow-

rumped warblers passed through the trees catching insects on the wing. They wore a gold spot on each breast, on their rumps, and on their crowns. Their white throats reminded me of the contour of a swallow's throat. The redstarts were thinking of housekeeping. The yellow-rumps were rangers, foraging on their line of march. In a few days the redstarts will have built the softest little cup in the crotch of a maple in that very grove ; the yellow-rumps will perhaps be north of the Basin of Minas.

Along the edges of the meadow, in alders and other low thick growth, bits of pure gold shot hither and thither in the sunlight. They were summer yellow-birds. " Sweety, sweety, sweet, sweet, sweet," is a free translation of their song. They, too, were love-making, and will soon be treasuring little spotted eggs in dainty fleece-lined, cup-shaped nests, built in those identical bushes. The Assabet will see their nests begun, but the leaves will grow large and keep the secret. Pine-creeping warblers and black-and-white creeping warblers are appropriately named. Both were abundant by the Assabet, and willing to be watched. They are inspectors of leaves and twigs, as the downy woodpeckers and little brown creepers are inspectors of trunks and limbs. All day long the trilling of the pine warblers sounded in the hot air. Seeing a handsome golden-olive male motionless on the lower limb of a pine, I crept close to him and lay on the fragrant needles watching him. For ten minutes neither he nor a chickadee in the next tree moved a feather. Then I whistled a gentle trill. The pine warbler stirred and listened. Then he tipped back his head, slightly opened his tiny beak and his throat trembled as the notes rolled evenly out. His notes roll: those of a chipping sparrow, which to the unpracticed ear are indistinguishable, are better indicated by a line of zigzags.

About one o'clock I crossed the Assabet and climbed a hill overlooking it and Boon Pond which empties into it. A strong breeze came like a benediction to make my lunch refreshing. Beyond the pond and the nearer hills I saw Nobscot Hill as many miles to the southeast of me in Stow, as it had been west of me in Wayland. Southward on a ridge was Marlborough. Northward in a hollow was Maynard, with its factory chimneys. There seemed to be some comfortable farming land in Stow, and that nearest us, and adjoining Honeypot Hill, — which, by the way, looked very insignificant from my nameless hill, which I liked because no one had advised me to climb it — was well ploughed, harrowed, and sown, and flanked by orchards and nurseries. On this cool hill-top white - throated sparrows were scratching in the leaves. There has been a great migration of these birds this year, or else the usual migration has seemed greater, because the birds have tarried during a week of cool, dry weather when they might have travelled quickly under different circumstances. Several of the apple-trees on the south side of this hill were in bloom, and the hum of bees came from them. It is a soothing sound, akin to the singing of a tea-kettle in some snug farmhouse kitchen. The orioles were in the orchard, but I watched in vain for humming birds. There were orioles in Cambridge on Saturday, but they were quiet; this day is their first of demonstration in numbers. It is also the first day of open lilac blossoms.

On the north shore of Boon Pond I found a large and beautiful grove of pines. A majority of the trees were pitch-pines, favorite resorts of birds at any season and in any weather. Lying on a bank deeply cushioned with pine needles I spent most of the afternoon fanned by a breeze which swept across the pond, listening to the music of the ripples, the warblers, and the field sparrows in the pasture beyond the grove, and gazing at the blue water, and the deep green of the foliage above me. In winter white-pines are very dark in color, while pitch-pines are golden-green. At this season, by mutual concessions, their coloring comes so nearly together that the eye finds difficulty in tracing their outlines. The pines were alive with warblers. Black-and-white creepers and pine warblers were most numerous, but black-throated greens, yellow-rumps, and yellow red-polls were almost always within sight or hearing. The trick of the yellow red-poll of wiggling his tail reminds me of the water thrush and the spotted sand-piper, but this bird certainly does not do it because he frequents the edges of waves or brooks. Between Boon Pond and the Assabet are some damp woods, a meadow and a line of willows. In the damp woods I found redstarts, black-throated blue warblers and an ovenbird. In the meadow a chewink was scratching among the grass and innocents, and in the willows summer yellow-birds, yellow-rumps, chestnut-sided warblers and black-throated greens caught flies on the wing and frolicked with each other among the falling blossoms. The blossoms as they fell upon the pond looked like yellow cater-pillars in danger of drowning, but as the wind caught them they sailed away merrily to distant shores. They made a brave fleet standing east-ward with all sails set. The ovenbird differs greatly from most of the other warblers. In fact, his character and dress both proclaim him a thrush. His back is olive-green, but it is not

far removed from the upper coloring of the
olive-backed thrush. Below he is white with
dusky spots on his breast and sides; and so is
the olive-backed thrush. His eyes are large and
earnest like a thrush's, and his nest is placed
upon the ground like that of the hermit thrush.
His dark orange crown set in black is his one
family emblem which a thrush would repudiate.
The ovenbird by the Assabet dropped to the
ground when he saw me and stole away as
slowly and silently as though he had been a
bittern, expert in the art of gliding.

At six o'clock, I stood on a low bridge over
the Assabet at Whitman's Crossing. The air
was full of swallows, the bushes and weeds were
rich in blackbirds, snowy and rose-tinted blossoms
decked the orchards, a fair pale sunset presided
over the sky and looked at itself in the river.
A snake with his head reared above the ripples
swam swiftly across from one weedy shore to the
other. The whistle of the train echoed a mile
away, and its growing thunder was in my ears.
Looking down the stream I could see a distant
hill; nearer were two wooded points, one on the
east, one on the west; nearer still a meadow full of
rank grass, and at my feet a mirror of blue
water. The coloring of that farewell glimpse of
Assabet was exquisite. The hill, covered probably with scrub oak, was rosy purple; of the

two wooded points, one was a mingling of the dark green of pines in shadow, the pale tender green of young beeches and birches, and the delicate reds of maples bearing their keys; the other, densely grown with alders, was rich with olive-browns and greens. The meadow grass was bluish green in shadow, and golden green in the sunlight. The intensity of the coloring seemed to be increased by looking at it with my head on one side. The effect of looking at any landscape in this way is to make it much like the image in a Claude Lorraine glass.

ROCK MEADOW AT NIGHT.

AT a quarter past six on Monday, May 11, I
caught a train at Porter's Station and went to
Belmont. A brisk walk along the Concord
turnpike, past blooming horse-chestnuts, and
through air heavy with the perfume of lilacs, over
Wellington Hill and down into Rock Meadow,
brought me just at sunset to the willows and the
home of the bittern. Turning into the marsh, I
crossed it on an old cart track to a wooded island
in its midst. I concealed myself among the
small trees on the edge of the island and swept
the meadow with my glass. Hundreds of frogs,
piping hylas, redwing blackbirds, crows, catbirds, and small birds mingled their voices in an
indescribable vesper chorus. Nature was alone.
Man's presence was unsuspected. I felt like an
intruder, but remembered that I had no evil in-
tent against anything in that great meadow.
While still searching with my glass for the bittern I heard his call, and at once discovered him.
He was a hundred yards from me in the grass.
He was facing northwest, and I was nearly

due north of him. His head, neck and shoulders were plainly visible. I settled myself into a comfortable position and watched him closely through my glass. Except when pumping or preparing to pump he was perfectly motionless, his beak pointing well upward. I knew when he was about to begin his music by the slow lowering of his beak. This was followed by the agitation of his breast and the first sounds from his throat. Then came his spasm, his neck and head being thrown up and snapped forward so violently that it seemed that the head must suffer dislocation. With these contortions came the noises which are so difficult to explain or describe. In this instance it seemed as though water was being shaken violently in a skin bottle. Listening intently, the sounds seemed best expressed by the syllables " kung-ka-unk," repeated three, four or five times. To the demoralization of my throat I repeated these syllables loudly, making them as nearly as possible as the bird did. He replied promptly and betrayed interest by more rapid and longer performances. This continued until it was so dark that I could only just discern him with my glass, when suddenly my attention was distracted by the sound of snipe flying overhead. Their performance is similar to that of the woodcock, but less elaborate. Rising to a considerable height above

the meadow, they fly with rapid wing-beats round
and round over it, making from time to time a
series of short notes, similar to those produced
by a person blowing in a rapidly intermittent
way across the mouth of a small shallow bottle.
Whether this noise is vocal or mechanical in
character, the bird controls it, and stops it without stopping its flight. This evening the bird
as a rule seemed satisfied with twenty-five or
thirty successive notes in a series.

My interest in the bittern was revived by
hearing him once more at a distance. Nothing
broke the level of the grass where his head had
been in sight so long. He seemed to have
moved quite rapidly over a space of a hundred
yards or more, and to be retreating westward
toward the woods and the brook. It was now
quite dark, save for the stars and a feeble young
moon in the western sky. The snipe were still
flying as I left the meadow and picked my way
carefully back to the turnpike. Their voices
and those of frogs and piping hylas alone disturbed the restful stillness of the night. I
looked up the road and down. It seemed like a
great conduit with light gleaming from both ends
along its white and level floor. Should I walk
to Belmont and wait for a ten o'clock train, or
traverse pastures and an unknown swamp in
order to reach Arlington Heights and later the

electric cars? There was novelty in the latter alternative, and I chose it.

Leaving Rock Meadow I crossed a field, then the road leading to the Belmont mineral spring, and entered a pasture. A number of cows were feeding by the light of the puny moon. They watched me suspiciously until the cedars concealed my hurrying form. Then I struck Marsh Street, and followed it uphill, until afar the tall electric light on the Heights flashed a message over intervening gloom. It was a mile distant. The first half of that mile was over land, or water, unknown to me. The second half was across the cedar-dotted pastures so often visited by me last winter. I left the road and struck into the unknown pasture, keeping the moon on my left and somewhat behind me. Cedars, pines, birches, well-armed barberry and blackberry bushes opposed my passage. Soon the land began to decline, the Arlington beacon was hidden, the air grew chilly, and the soil moist and soft. Then patches of water gleamed on my left, and the voices of frogs greeted me. A shaky stone wall was crossed, and the dry land turned to mud and tussocks of grass. Then came a ditch. This proved the crisis in the walk, for beyond it the land rose and soon I reached familiar ground. I recognized cedars which had suffered in the ice and snow storms of January. Their backs were still bent. On my right were the dark woods in which I had found the most beautiful snow caverns, and near by was the ground frequented during long cold weeks by the flock of winter robins. The soft May night, with its frog music, was unlike those days of hyperborean delights. It was more comfortable and more commonplace. The next stone wall was the one where snow fleas had swarmed by millions. I recalled in one of its angles the white snow bearing the footprints of quail and field mice. So I went on, picking my way cautiously over the dark ground until I came out into Park Avenue, close by the Heights.

The view from the Heights at night is bewitching. Myriads of stars people the blue heavens, and myriads of baser stars people those depths below. The stars above differ one from another in glory; the stars below differ one from another in evil. Those above tell of eternity and rest. Those below tell of toil, vanity, self-indulgence, crime, sickness, — the unrest of human life. Still, being a man, I looked down into that sea of light, and seemed to find one star gleaming in the distance which was a part of the glory above, and related only by propinquity to the evil of the city. Towards that light I took my way, and finding it, put it out and went to bed.

THE SECRETS OF THE MEADOW.

THERE are days in May when the northwest wind sweeps through the trees with the blustering rush of September air. It seems to be testing the young foliage and warning the soft, glossy, newly unfolded leaves of the fate which attends them only a few weeks later in the year. It is rough with the apple blossoms piled high upon the orchard's open arms, and it waves to and fro the "Christmas candles" of the horse-chestnut trees. On its breath is wafted the perfume of lilacs, or the pungent message of pine woods burning, in spots left too long dry by the fickle spring rains. There is a chill in this turbulent air, not the damp chill of the east wind, but the chill which has in it a faint suggestion of autumnal frosts. Even after the wind goes to sleep at sunset the air remains cold, and farmers wonder if there is to be a late frost.

Sunday, May 17, was such a day, and, as the woods were too full of noise and waving leaves for birds to be either heard or seen, my friend and I went to Rock Meadow to visit my bittern. We reached the willows at four in the afternoon, feeling sure he would be present, because his mate is undoubtedly somewhere in that quiet land of waving marsh grass, keeping warm her four or five drab eggs in her cunningly concealed nest. Between the wind gusts we listened intently to hear his now familiar note. He was not in the place where I had seen him before, but at half past four, as we reached the northern part of the meadow, I distinctly heard his booming near at hand. We crept cautiously along the line of wall and bushes bounding the meadow on the north. Suddenly my friend gripped me by the shoulder and dragged me to the ground. A pair of black ducks flew by, scudding low over the bushes. We next disturbed a flock of twenty crows, which rose from an old cornfield where they had been feeding. Rock Meadow is a remarkable rendezvous for crows, summer and winter. What makes it so attractive I have thus far been unable to ascertain. These crows kept close watch upon us the rest of the afternoon.

Standing upon a knoll capped with a few barberry bushes, we looked straight down the whole length of Rock Meadow. The rains of the past two days had given a wonderful impetus to the grass, which was now high enough to hide a bittern completely, unless he chose to raise his slender neck above it. With our glasses we swept the wind - ruffled grass land thoroughly over and over again. The bittern was not to be seen. But almost at once my friend whispered excitedly, "I see him," and by a common impulse we merged our outlines in those of the barberries behind us. The wary bird was in the edge of the meadow, at the foot of the slight slope on which we stood. His head and neck were raised above the grass, and resembled in size and color a cat-tail, which the wind and weather had reduced to a mass of flaxen seed-vessels loosely attached to their stalks. For several minutes he did not move, and with our eyes glued to the barrels of our field-glasses we watched his uplifted beak and stiffened neck. Slowly his head dropped, and with a premonitory shake disappeared in the grass. Seven seconds after it was flung up, so that the bill pointed to the sky, but it fell back as quickly into the grass. This was done four times, and each time the "kung-ka-unk" came to our ears. After this performance had been repeated several times, the bittern sank slowly beneath the grass, as though to begin pumping, but did not reappear. Waiting for a while, we walked a few rods along the edge of the meadow to a point where several oak trees spread their strong arms to the breeze. Concealed behind their trunks, we watched the sea of grass, and soon discovered the beak and

long stiffened neck of the bittern pointing
towards the zenith, from a spot fifteen or twenty
yards distant from the place which we had just
left.   He was quite as near us as before, and
this time he had no suspicion of our where-
abouts.   I climbed into the middle of one of the
oaks, and my friend secured a comfortable position on the wall below, and with glasses and a
stop-watch in constant use, we reduced the bittern's performance to its lowest terms.

The bird, when at rest between his spasms,
stood with his neck extended and raised, and his
head and beak pointing forward and upward.
The first indication that he was about to pump
was a deliberate lowering of his beak to the
level of his body, and the settling down into his
breast and feathers of his long neck.   This made
his breast look larger and fuller than when his
head was raised and his neck stretched upward.
The slow motion of lowering the head into line
with the body was followed by a slight shake of
the head and throat, and the first of a series of
motions which were caused apparently by volun-
tary swallowing of air.   The bill opened, the
head was raised slightly and then dropped, and
the bill closed with a snap.   The first snap was
scarcely audible, the second was much louder,
the third, fourth, fifth, and sixth perfectly distinct, and a seventh, when made, was less dis-

tinct, partly because instantly followed by the
first "pump." Usually six or seven snaps were
succeeded by three or four pumps, but the bird
varied the number of snaps and pumps consider-
ably, and I presume different bitterns would show
marked individualities. By a "pump" I mean
the triple sound which is called "booming,"
"stakedriving," or "pumping," according to the
fancy of the writer, and which to my ears sounds
as much like "kung-ka-unk" as anything else.
The head is in a line with the back when the
"kung" is made, but as the first syllable reaches
the ears of an observer, he sees the bird's head
flung abruptly and sharply back, so that the bill
points for a second to the zenith, and then sees
it thrown down again to its former position.
The "ka-unk" follows this spasm so closely that
it is impossible to be certain whether the "ka" is
made on the upward stroke or on the downward.
The three sounds "kung-ka-unk" occupy just
about a second of time, which makes it clear
how rapid is the motion of the head. The
period from the instant that the head first
reaches the level of the back to the instant when
the fourth "unk" makes the end of the song, is
in most cases exactly ten seconds in duration.
Then the head is raised, the long neck extends
itself, the breast grows smaller accordingly, and
the bird resumes his stiffness and watchfulness.

My friend's stop-watch recorded thirty-seven seconds as the normal interval between the last pump of one performance and the first snap of the succeeding one. Twice during an hour the bittern sank beneath the grass and glided to a new spot. Once I caught a glimpse of him on his way, and he seemed to be moving more rapidly than the duration of his concealment indicated. From his third station he took flight, and, with long, graceful wing - strokes, flew an eighth of a mile down the meadow and alighted on the exact spot in which I had found him the Monday evening preceding. We hastened back to the turnpike and sought the cover I had previously used. As we listened to the bird at a distance, with a grove of trees interrupting his notes, the only sound which we could hear was the " ka," which, under the changed conditions became the true stake-driving " chuck " or " tock." The nearer we came to the bird, the less there remained of this acoustic metamorphosis, and as we crawled cautiously through the woods to the edge of the swamp nearest him it disappeared altogether, and to our ears the " kung-ka-unk " was as distinct as before. We listened to and watched the strange genius of the marsh until he stopped his performance at twenty minutes of eight ; but our thoughts were at times diverted from him.

A short-billed marsh wren sang his quaint, nervous, and unmusical little song to us. It seemed to me, never having heard it before, that it was a sound well calculated not to be heard by any ears but those specially attuned to it. A similar thought had occurred to me earlier in the afternoon, when my friend called my attention to what he called the " background music " of the crickets, audible probably that day for the first time this year. They are sounds which go to form the great undertone of the day, and the ear is usually too busy with more distinctly separated and louder sounds to take note of them. Let, however, the rest of the world's noises cease, or the listener become feverish and over sensitive to sound, and this " background music " surges into the brain like an incoming tide and thrills every nerve with its rapid rhythm.

A sound which even a deaf man could not have ignored that evening was the persistent quacking, or rather quaarking, of a male black duck, who was exploring a ditch between us and the bittern. His better-half was near by, although silent, and I hope for her sake that his voice was more musical in her ears than in ours. After traversing the ditch the ducks flew, the male still bawling at his wife while in the air. It was not more than ten minutes before they returned, the drake quaarking, and plumped down into a small pool near by.

At ten minutes of eight, as we left the meadow and strolled towards our waiting carryall, the upper air resounded with the strange music of the flying snipe. My friend, who has heard this sound scores of times, feels confident that it is mechanical in character,—" drumming," in fact. To my ears it seems to be vocal in quality. Whichever it may be, its weird sweetness makes it one of the most attractive night or twilight sounds in nature. One accepts rather as a matter of course the sunlight singing of a light-hearted little finch or vireo, but for a shy recluse of the swamps to betake himself at evening to the heights of the sky, and there against the stars, invisible to all except the keenest eyes, to produce his witching serenade, is something unique, and captivating to the imagination.

Early in the day Rock Meadow told us two secrets which were very precious to two families of birds. In the great pollard willows which line the causeway are many comfortable crotches, angles and curves which appeal to nest builders. In one of these a robin had placed her nest and laid her eggs. Her bright eye watched us keenly as we drew near the tree, and the moment she felt the force of our gaze upon her, she slipped away to reproach us from a distance. Those greenish blue eggs were the first I had seen this year, and they seemed like precious

stones, so delicate were they in form and color.
The willows have also many caverns of various
sizes and shapes in their trunks. From one of
these, through which and to the depths of which
a man's hand could but just pass, a song sparrow
sprang as we sauntered past. Fortunate for her
that we were friends, for in the cave from which
she came lay her five richly decorated eggs. As
a rule this sparrow builds a grass nest by a
brook bank, flat on the pasture turf, in a low
evergreen in a meadow, or in a cup-shaped hollow in a decaying stump. Among all the song
sparrows' nests which my friend and I had seen,
none approached this in the security and origi-
nality of its location.

By starting from Cambridge at half-past six
A. M., on Saturday, May 23d, I was able to leave
Fitchburg at nine behind an eccentric stable
horse, bound for the top of Wachusett Mountain. The distance to the foot of the mountain
was about nine miles. For the first four miles
the road was far from agreeable. We encountered rough pavements or dust, the obtrusive
features of a young and by no means beautiful
city, hillsides denuded of trees, and in many
cases turned into quarries, the Nashua River
defiled by mill-waste and stained by chemicals,
railroad embankments coated with ashes and bare
of verdure, and brick mill buildings, grim, noisy,
and forbidding. The road gradually ascended,
and at length crossed the river, passed under
the railway and sought the woods. A parting
glance down stream showed a mass of steeples,
chimneys, brick walls, quarry derricks, freight
cars, and dirty mill ponds flanked by wasted hillsides and overhung by a cloud of smoke. Between the smoke and the hurly-burly of the
town a distant line of hills shone out on the

horizon. It was a promise of something purer above.

As we followed the highway southward toward Princeton we passed through no forests or remnants of forest, nothing but cleared land or new woodland in which birch, poplar, cherry, and other inferior growth predominated. The undergrowth was mainly mountain laurel, which a month from now will be a joy to the eye. Warblers sang in every thicket — the ovenbirds being especially noisy. Next to them the sweet but wearisome voice of the red-eyed vireo sounded on all sides. Brown thrushes were noticeably numerous and tame. Along the wayside, lady's slipper, white and purple violets, hawthorn, clintonia, blackberry vines and barberry bushes, painted trillium, chokeberry and chokecherry, star flower, and houstonia were abundant. The great size of the dandelions attracted our notice, and the violets were unusually large and beautiful.

A little after eleven o'clock we emerged from between two ridges and saw the mass of Wachusett before us. A long even slope from northwest to southeast terminated in a flat summit, on which several wooden buildings stood out sharply and disagreeably against the sky. The southeastern slope was much more abrupt than the northwestern, but far from precipitous. There was

nothing grand or impressive about the mountain
apart from the simple fact of its height, two
thousand feet. The carriage road to the summit proceeds part way along the eastern base,
then meets a road from Princeton and turns
abruptly northwestward, makes several great
serpent curves upon the northern and northwestern face, and finally gains the summit from
the east. The road is remarkably well surveyed, and is kept in good order. The eccentric stable horse, which up to the moment of
our reaching the ascent had shown a willingness
to go anywhere but to the mountain, started up
the slope with such zeal that I found it impossible to keep up with him on foot. This made
our progress rather more rapid than pleasant,
and the charming glimpses of scenery below us
and at a distance were only half appreciated.
Most of the trees on the mountain seemed to be
of recent growth, but among them dozens of
scattered giants rose to show what lumbermen's
greed might have left in the way of a forest if
it had been restrained. Some of these large
trees were sugar-maples, while others were yellow
birches and beeches. The most striking flowers
along the mountain road were creamy white
bunches of early elder, pinkish purple rhodora,
and rose-colored azalea just coming into bloom.

Birds were few and far between on the mountain sides, although they had been plenty below. The call of the ovenbird occasionally reached our ears, and at one point the scolding of a superb scarlet tanager drew our eyes to the spot where his plumage seemed burning among the leaves.

The summit, reached just at noon, proved anything but attractive. Stripped of trees and bushes, it has been afflicted by a large and commonplace hotel, several barns and ugly sheds, and a bowling alley, billiard room, and tintype gallery. The north wind was polluted by the escaping odors of a cask of gasoline, and when we sought the groves below the crest, we encountered tin cans, broken bottles and other remains of previous seasons. When one seeks gasoline, electric bells, and a tintype gallery he has a right to feel pleased on finding them, but when I seek Nature on a mountain top and find her fettered by civilization, I have a right to feel aggrieved. However, we endeavored to forget man and his gasoline in the contemplation of the beautiful.

What first struck us was the number of fires which were contributing columns of blue smoke to an atmosphere already dimmed by its thin strata. More than a dozen such fires were in sight. Thanks to them, the view was soft and dreamy in tone, giving the idea of distance more by suggestion than by disclosure. Eastward and southward, where the smoke lay heaviest, the land seemed flat. Most of it was free from forest, but every few miles a dark line or spot told of a grove of pines saved thus far from the destroying hand of this generation of timber thieves. A few lakes caught the light of the sky and flashed it back to us, and scattered houses, usually white, broke the monotony of green fields and pastures. Marlborough on the east, Worcester on the south, Gardner on the west, and Fitchburg on the north were nuclei of houses, reminding me of the piles of sand which form themselves on a pane of sanded glass when a violin bow is drawn across its edge. Far away in the smoke on the western horizon rose the Berkshire Hills with proud Greylock dominant over them. I thought of the fair Connecticut flowing southward between them and us, and of the bright Hudson rolling beyond them on its journey toward the modern Babylon. Northward of the Berkshires the sky line was ragged with hills and distant mountains in Vermont and New Hampshire, even to the point where, rising serenely from its granite bed, Monadnock reared its noble head toward the heavens. It alone in all that smoky landscape was majestic. All else was soft, yielding, sleepy, but Monadnock rose with clear-cut out-

lines and sharp summit, attracting the eye, fix-
ing the attention, compelling admiration. On
its right — that is, to the eastward — its pack
strung out in perpetual pursuit of it. There
was Peterborough in the fore and the Uncanoonucs far behind, Crotchett Mountain in the
north and Watatic in the south — the latter
" out of bounds," if the laws of this great chase
require the pursuing hills to stay on New
Hampshire soil. In the dim distance, beyond
this group of sunny hills, hallowed in my mind
by a thousand loving recollections of boyhood
days, were other hills. What were they? I
could not tell beyond the certainty that they
were stepping stones to that far northland
which I call home, Kearsarge, Cardigan, Cube,
Moosilauke, Stinson, Ossipee, Chocorua! I
could recall the feeling of every summit under
my weary foot, as I had pressed upon it with the
satisfaction of a conqueror. Perhaps in a clear
day some of those sentinel peaks of New Hampshire can be really recognized from Wachusett.

After absorbing the beauties of the distant
view we explored the stunted groves of beeches
and oaks, mountain ash, striped and mountain
maples below the summit. Here I found a robin,
on a nest containing three eggs. The dwarfed
trees, being numerous and well proportioned,
seemed of normal size, but the bird, her nest

and I appeared to have expanded beyond our proper dimensions. The carpet under this grove was woven of beautiful forms. Its warp was of arbutus, false Solomon seal, checkerberry, strawberry, and potentilla, its woof of clintonia, hobble bush, sarsaparilla, skunk currant, twisted stalk, and columbine.

The arbutus was heavily laden with flowers which had spent their sweetness on birds and breezes. They were dry, and their lovely tints had changed to chestnut and russet. A great bed of anemones rippled in the wind. They seemed to be four weeks behind their sisters, which I had found so abundant at Heard's Island. In a low tree above them a junco called to his mate, and I felt confident that this mountain top had seemed to them a comfortable nesting spot. Two thousand feet upward is almost as good as two hundred miles northward. The Nashville warblers which I saw on or near the summit seemed also to agree to this principle.

At half-past two we started down the mountain, and although our eccentric horse was even more anxious to go down than to go up, we succeeded in seeing more of the view than while ascending. At the foot of the north slope of the mountain lay Wachusett Pond, a charming sheet of water, reminding me by its location and

size of Dublin Pond, nestling at the north of
Monadnock. Over it, beyond a multitude of
farms, groves, and hills, Monadnock cut into the
sky as the commanding feature of the sleepy
landscape. This combination of lake and mountain was the most beautiful view Wachusett
gave us. Although the summit of the mountain remained springlike, the lowlands along
the Nashua River were burned deeply with the
brand of summer. Early flowers had gone,
later ones were going. Migrant birds had
mainly gone by, and the dry z-z-z-z-z-z-z-z of the
blackpoll warbler wore on the edge of one's
temper much as the song of the harvest fly does
in its season. There are many pleasant views
from the Fitchburg train as it hurries along from
the valley of the Nashua across that of the
Assabet and Musketaquid to that of the Charles :
Wachusett across the vale of Leominster, Assabet water at Concord Junction, the meadows
of the Sudbury above Concord, the level fields
which Emerson loved, Fairhaven Hill and
Walden Pond where Thoreau studied life and
its mysteries, Stony Brook, the Charles at Waltham, Waverley Oaks ; and then, across the
Belmont marshes, Memorial and Mt. Auburn
Towers, the emblems of eager life and the rest
which eager life has no need to fear.

ONE of the fairest spots known to me in the neighborhood of Cambridge is the "Wren Orchard." Thither on the morning of this Sunday, May 24, I took my little covey of buttercup hunters. The orchard was set out several generations ago, and not only the unknown hand which planted it but the house that sheltered him and his have passed away forever. The ground where the orchard stands is a hillside facing the south. Summer and winter the sun watches over it and only gentle winds sweep across it. North and east of this sunny Eden are elms which shut it out from inquisitive distance. Westward it is guarded by dark cedars, and along its southern edge rise rank upon rank of great oaks and chestnuts, in whose midst is a small swamp overhung by ancient willows. The swamp is made by a gentle brook which begins life in the elm grove north of the orchard, spends all its days murmuring over a pebbly bed among forget-me-nots and violets, and which crosses the orchard at its middle. The orchard and its borders contain

high land, low land, dry land, wet land, open
land, wooded land, hard wood, soft wood, evergreen wood and apple wood — all the elements
of home and shelter which a majority of land
birds desire. No wonder then that summer and
winter the wren orchard is alive with birds.
As I write these words merry calls and music
come from all its quarters in pleasing medley.
Many of the birds have nests near by, others are
building or planning where to place their nests.
The latest migrants are now here. In the low
land south of the orchard I hear a blackbilled
cuckoo, saying "Coo-coo-coo, coo-coo-coo, coo-
coo-coo-coo, coo-coo-coo-coo." In the largest of
the elms east of the orchard an indigo bird is
singing his clear and joyous notes. His coloring
is as intense as that of a scarlet tanager which I
have been watching in the highest branches of a
great oak. Another late migrant, whose voice
is in my ears, is the wood pewee. His notes,
like most of the sounds made by the tyrant flycatchers, are querulous and unmusical. He
seems to be continually complaining that insects
will not fly into his mouth.

The thrush family inhabits this orchard in
numbers. Robins build in the apple-trees, —
a nest with four eggs in it is in the tree next me,
— catbirds and brown thrushes dwell in the
clumps and hedges of barberry bushes with

which the orchard abounds, and the mild-eyed veery lives near the swampy spot by the great willows. All of these singers have been pouring out their notes during the past hour.

While my little buttercup hunters have been gathering great fistfuls of pure golden blossoms, the turf of the orchard has not been wholly theirs. Among a herd of a dozen deer-like Jersey heifers six cowbirds have been walking about catching flies ; chipping and song - sparrows have hopped about in the grass ; robins, thrushes, and bluebirds have found worms in the earth, and I suspect that a great glossy crow who seems to have a nest in a high tree in the swamp has found something edible while stalking up and down the brookside. From the thick woods to the south comes every now and then the clear " bob-white " of the quail, and they are near enough for me to hear the low " bob " which precedes the loud " bob " in their three-syllabled whistle.

I brought two wicker baskets to-day, one containing milk, sandwiches, and strawberries, and the other a distinguished and important member of my household. His name is Puffy, and he now sits on the dead limb of an apple-tree, his great dark eyes solemnly gazing at a redstart, who is abusing him from a neighboring limb. His brown and white feathers blend so well with the rough bark of the apple tree that it requires sharp or experienced eyes to see him. Puffy is one of two barred owls which I have held in happy captivity since June 1, 1888, the day on which I took them from their ancestral castle in a White Mountain forest. Puffy is not a favorite with other birds. They dislike and distrust him, and when I place him in a tree, from which a crippled wing prevents his flying, they come to him in dozens, scolding and complaining at his very existence in their midst. To-day, while the last petals of the apple blossoms have been falling around him, most of the birds already named, and in addition kingbirds, least flycatchers, redstarts, black-and-white creepers, ovenbirds, black-throated green warblers, red-eyed and solitary vireos, downy and golden-winged woodpeckers, rose-breasted grosbeaks and chickadees have perched or hovered near, noisily expressing their bitter feelings towards him. Sometimes I see his great round head turned towards the sky, and his eyes fix themselves upon some moving bird. A chimney swift or a barn swallow attracts him for a second only, but if a hawk or a crow crosses his heavens his eyes never leave it until it disappears from view. He cares little or nothing for the abuse of other birds, but if they actually assault him, as kingbirds and flickers often do, his serenity is marred. It is still a little early in the season for birds to become frantic at his presence. When the robins, vireos, and chickadees have tender young dependent on them, the sight of Puffy will drive them into paroxysms of rage.

I have called this warm pasture flecked with buttercups and fallen apple petals the " Wren Orchard." It deserves the name, for it is the only spot in New England that I have ever visited where house wrens survive and build regularly. Even now I hear the jingling notes of this once common but now rare bird falling like drops of water from a fountain through the sunlit air. Two years ago (May 26, 1889) I found one of their nests. Attracted by the showery notes of the male I crept into a corner of the orchard, where an old apple - tree grew alone in a circle of privet and barberry bushes. Concealed under their branches I watched the tree. Soon a wren appeared, then disappeared in the substance of the tree. Its tiny body seemed to melt into the bark of a horizontal limb about twelve feet above the ground. I examined this limb, seeking a hole in it, but found none. After a second period of watching I saw that the bird passed into the limb by a hole on its under side. I climbed the tree, measured the extent of the hole, which was seven or eight inches, and then cut a neat door into it from above. There on a mass of soft shredded bark and odds and ends of forest fibre lay seven tiny eggs. They were round little eggs, having a salmon-white groundwork thickly and uniformly covered with hundreds of minute reddish brown spots.

Bluebirds also build in this orchard, and so do downy woodpeckers, flickers, and chickadees; all birds which rear their families in the hollows of trees. A bluebird's nest which I found here was placed at the bottom of a dark dry cavity in an apple trunk. The hole was large enough for a somewhat slender hand to pass through, and so deep that half the forearm was in the hole before the eggs could be touched. Once in a while the bluebird lays pure white eggs, but generally they are pale blue, and to an unpracticed eye might suggest a reflection of the sky in a pool of rain water at the bottom of the hole. Almost all birds which nest in hollow trees lay unmarked white eggs.

While I am writing a downy woodpecker and a flicker both make their voices heard in the orchard.

The barberry bushes are in bloom to-day, and I have amused my buttercup hunters by showing them how the barberry flowers set traps for their insect visitors. As one turns up the yellow

cup of the flower and looks into it, he sees the
stamens pressed against the inner curve of the
petals and away from the central column of the
pistil. If a straw be gently pressed upon the
base of the stamens the latter jump forward and
clasp it tightly enough to hold it. This pressure covers the embraced surface with yellow
pollen, and in the case of an insect would make
it perfectly certain that in shaking himself free
he would not only rub some of the pollen upon
the pistils of the flower he was in, but that he
would bear away enough of it to cross-fertilize
the next blossom he entered.

I can hear the songs of a robin, an oriole, and
a rose-breasted grosbeak. They have marked
differences, yet I find many people are unable to
distinguish them unaided. A thrush, a starling,
and a finch should not sing alike, but in Cambridge the three birds build in the same trees,
and mingle in their daily lives so constantly that
it is possible they have learned to speak alike.
The robin's song is animated, but rough and
full of harsh passages. It reminds me of a
farmer's boy bellowing his favorite tune as he
drives his oxen home through a wood road.
The oriole often makes music, but his voice is
apt to crack and flat until his silence seems
golden. The grosbeak sings the robin's theme
with all the robin's spirit, but without the

robin's harshness. It is a stirring, bold, free
song, having little musical merit and no pathos,
but plenty of " go " and " swing." The metallic
squeak which the bird generally makes just
before he begins his song is an odd and unmis-
takable sound, which once learned never fails to
identify this beautiful finch.

Back of the orchard in the evergreens I hear a
chickadee calling, and a moment ago a blue jay's
scream attracted my notice. Their voices carry
me back many Sundays to those winter days
when I began my walks. This slope now soft with
thick grass and splendid with golden buttercups,
shy violets, jolly little potentillas and pale wild
geraniums swaying in the breeze, was then
eighteen inches deep in snow. These trees now
arrayed in lustrous foliage were then encased in
ice armor or muffled in the snow which crushed
the cedars to the earth and wrecked yonder
prostrate willow, whose fall I remember seeing
and hearing. The blue jays, chickadees, and
robins which frequented this warm pasture in
January are probably hundreds of miles from
here to-day, rearing their young in the woods
and fields of the far north. The glistening snow
which then burdened the earth and trees is now
gleaming in this brook, flowing as life blood
through these tree trunks, forming the chief
part of these brightly tinted leaves of grass,

ferns, brakes, flowers and shrubs, or floating
high in that warm sky, and as a pure spirit of
the past smiling upon the land of plenty to
which it never was unfriendly or unkind. Yes,
the winter has melted into spring and now the
spring has blossomed into summer. Nature,
once so cold and white and still, is now warm,
gleaming with many tints and trembling with
growth in every marvellous group of its restless
molecules. The tide of life was ebbing in
January. Now it is nearing the flood. Then
the soul of man needed courage and faith to
make it believe that the frozen world had un-
quenchable life, persistent force, locked up in it.
Now the soul needs the intelligence of God to
enable it to count the wonders of realization
which burning life and exuberant energy have
placed above, below, and on every side.

As I look at this grass and the flowers which
shine in its midst, at the myriad leaves upon the
trees, at the butterflies, caterpillars, locusts, ants,
and bees, and at the birds, solicitous for their
eggs or young, should I be sorrowful because
in a few days the annual tide of life will turn
and the grass begin to ripen, the flowers to fade,
the butterflies to die, and the birds to take note
of the sky and begin their journey southward?
No. The rhythm of the universe demands just
this coming and going, rising and falling, ex-

panding and contracting, living and dying.
Without reaction there could be no action.
Without death we should not know what life
meant; without what we call sorrow there could
be no joy.

I hear the song of the veery down there under
the willows. It is a weird, ventriloquial song.
The bird seems making its gypsy music to
itself, not to the world. In that dark corner
the trillium grows, keeping its face hidden under its cloak. There, too, the jack-in-the-
pulpit is found masking its face. The song of
the veery has in it the tinkling of bells, the
jangle of the tamborine. It recalls to me the
gypsy chorus in the "Bohemian Girl," and when
I hear it as evening draws on, I can picture light
feet tripping over the damp grass, and in the
shadows made by moving of branches and ferns
I can see dark forms moving back and forth in
the windings of the dance.

A MAY rain after a spring drought has a wonderfully reviving effect upon the landscape. It washes away dust, expands tissues, intensifies colors, deepens shadows and heightens contrasts; fills the brooks, and veils the horizon in white mist. On May 29, just after the sun, presumably in rubber boots and a mackintosh, had crossed the meridian, a train rolled out of Boston, bound for the north. Its windows were soon wet and covered with coal ashes. Raindrops were driven at all angles across them, distorting the landscape and discouraging observation. The rain accompanied the train to the end of its journey. It beat upon the Saugus marshes and the sands of Revere Beach, and it splashed into the rushing tide of the Merrimac flowing seaward at Newburyport. The Hampton marshes were strikingly picturesque in the storm. Near the train the lush grass on the flats could be seen bowing before the gusts. The tide-rivers and channels were full to their brim, and showed snowy white under the colorless sky and between their verdant banks. Within their meshes and reaching on to the invisible sea, were thousands of acres of green marsh dotted with haystacks, or the round groups of piles from which the stacked hay had been removed. The most distant stacks looked no larger than thimbles, and were dim in the fast falling rain. As the train sped over the marshes these distant haycocks seemed to move as little as the sun would have, had it been hurrying on that far line of sky, while the near ones swung swiftly past, and those intermediate went with them, yet more slowly. The marsh seemed like a great wheel revolving beside us, its lines of haycocks being the innumerable spokes forever whirling past.

The rain pelted the Piscataqua at Portsmouth, and almost hid the great ship-houses at the Kittery Navy Yard. It was beating upon Milton ponds as the train rolled past them, and it was swelling the flood of Bearcamp water as we gained Ossipee valley. Of course no mountains were to be seen. They were hidden in the rolling masses of vapor which filled the upper air. Towards them, however, and into their midst we continued our journey by stage. The trees were dripping with rain, patches of mist trailed westward over the hill-tops, the bushes and flowers by the roadside glistened with moisture. In places the air was heavy with the spicy breath of the choke-cherry, whose multitudes of finger-

shaped racemes drooped under the weight of
rain. The perfume of this tree is, at certain distances, akin to that of the heliotrope. White
and purple violets, star-flower, chokeberry, false
solomon's seal, fringed polygala, and dwarf cornel
blossomed by thousands on every side. Brakes
were just opening, many being still coiled, waiting some elfin touch to expand, but the ferns
were present in force. They are one of the
triumphs of nature. Numerous in species, exquisite in form, tender in color, graceful in motion, harmless in growth, wholesome in odor, sensitive yet persistent, refined yet abundant. Some
of them perish at the first frost, as for example
the onoclea; others like the Christmas-fern and
polypody remain green and buoyant all winter,
even when half buried in snow or covered by ice.
The coloring of the *osmunda regalis* as it un-
folds is in beautiful contrast to that of the other
osmundas, the former being light red, salmon
colored, orange, or even bright red, and the latter silvery green. Bird voices were not quenched
by the rain. The harsh squawk of the night-hawk
came from the mist; hermit thrushes sang in
damp balsam cloisters, chimney swifts sprinkled
the air with their small notes, and the thin voices
of warblers were heard in every thicket. Here,
as in Cambridge, the migration seemed to be
over and resident species present in full force.

The stage turned into a narrow ribbon road
lined with white-stemmed birches. The road
pointed straight towards Chocorua, whose vast
base rose like a wall across the north, meeting
the even line of white cloud which concealed its
peak. To the right, glimpses of water revealed
the position of Chocorua Lake. The ribbon
road led to a red-roofed cottage in the midst of
an ancient orchard, and there stopped. This cottage stands within the limits of the wilderness.
In winter the snow lies around it in deep drifts,
and for many weeks at a time no snowshoe
leaves its latticed imprint near. The mountain broods over it, and when in cold nights the
groaning of the ice gives the lake voice, it tells
the cottage the story of its journey from the sky
and its plans for reaching the sea. From the
days after the civil war until five years ago, this
cottage was the home of the children of the
forest. Man left it to be shingled by lichens
and glazed by cobwebs. Snow lay deep in its
attic, pewees nested in the angles of its rooms,
snakes and skunks dwelt in its foundations,
generations of swifts were hatched in its chimney, and chipmunks frolicked in its empty rooms.
To the deer, the crow, the fox, and the hedgehog, this house had no terrors. It had ceased
to belong to man. Although of late years it
has been my home, I have done what I can to

maintain the belief among the creatures of the forest that it belongs to them.

It was seven o'clock as the stage rolled up to the cottage door, left us, turned around and departed.   Inside, a fire blazed on the old hearth, and the bark on the birch logs sputtered and crackled like burning fat.   Outside, the rain fell softly, making a pleasant murmur on the leaves, a murmur which blended with the voices of crickets, tree toads, hylas, and frogs.   As night fell and the fire burned low, the clock and the whippoorwills began a conversation which lasted long, perhaps till morning.

A rainy morning does not discourage birds. They are just as hungry, and almost if not quite as tuneful as on other days.   The morning of the 30th of May was warm and wet, but the air was as full of bird notes as of rain drops.   A white-throated sparrow sang *pea-pea-peabody, peabody, peabody,* under my window ; a cat-bird in the grape-vine in front of the house revelled in a medley of notes, hermit thrushes rendered their sweet phrases from three neighboring groves, and red-eyed vireos, chestnut-sided warblers, redstarts, ovenbirds, barn-swallows, and swifts filled in any gaps with their joyous voices. A pair of catbirds were building their nests in the lilac bush at the corner of the cottage, so near a window that a long arm could reach it.   The

pewees were feeding their young in a nest at
the top of a pilaster under the eaves of the
house. The piazza rail was their perch all
through the day. They have occupied the nest
three years. The nest used in 1888 is in an angle
of the roof near by. The pewee has a trick
which it is hard to explain. It jerks its tail upward sharply about once in two seconds. The
motion is petulant in character, but suggestive
of eternal vigilance. Both birds caught insects
for their young, and the feeding process seemed
perpetual. Over the dairy window is a wooden
gutter to catch the rain from the roof. This
being a dry spring, a foolish robin built in the
gutter, near its lower end. The nest was soaked
by the storm on the 29th and 30th, and partly
dissolved by the trickling water, but the robin
stuck to her eggs. The noisiest birds anywhere
near the cottage were a pair of great-crested flycatchers. They screamed or whistled all day.
Their voices are harsh, their tempers and manners bad, but their nesting habits are very interesting. They build every year in the hollow of
an apple tree, where a large limb broke off long
ago and gave the elements a chance to make a
deep, dark cavity. The last nest I examined
consisted of cow's hair, reddish fur, feathers, a
squirrel's tail, grasses, dry leaves, shreds of birch
bark, and many small pieces of snake-skin. One

year nearly the whole of a discarded snake-skin was placed in a circle around the eggs. I have yet to find one of their nests without a piece of snake-skin in it. I think the bird uses it because experiments tried by previous generations have shown that the skin is useful in scaring away squirrels, mice, and other enemies. Between the cottage and the lake I found a song sparrow's nest. It was built in marked contrast to the one in the willow tree on Concord turnpike. Flat on the ground at the edge of a ditch, its only shelter was a bunch of brush, cut last season and left to dry. From above, the nest and its contents were perfectly concealed, but by stooping down and looking in from the bank of the ditch I could see the neat grass cup and its four richly colored eggs. The bird in leaving the nest showed herself expert in dodging. She glided from beneath the brush and over the edge of the ditch, much as a leaf might have if impelled by the wind. Dropping to the bottom of the trench she ran down its gravelly bottom nearly to the shore of the lake before she took wing for the woods. Although the chipping sparrow spends most of its summer in the grass, it builds its nest of coiled horse-hair in the branch of an apple-tree, at least eight or ten feet from the ground. One of their nests was nearly finished in a tree near the dining-room window.

The swifts had not begun building in the chimney, but the cause of their delay was discovered when one of them was found beating against the inside of an upstairs chamber window. The poor frightened creature had come down the chimney into the fireplace, and had probably been a captive for several days. Holding it gently but firmly in my left hand, I endeavored to hypnotize it, as I had the peabody bird on April 30th. Its brown eyes looked at me beseechingly, and it winced whenever I touched it. Its flat head, tiny beak leading to a wide mouth, long slender wings, insignificant feet and legs, and strange little tail, with bare spikes at the tips of the feathers, combined to form a creature more like a living arrow than a denizen of earth. Taking it out-of-doors I caressed it a moment more and then slowly opened my fingers. Could it be that the tiny being, which I might have crushed by one grip of my hand, possessed a speed almost equal to a projectile, and a brain powerful enough to will that speed and to direct it?´ Like a breath the bird was gone. Those slender wings throbbing through the air bore it higher and higher, round and round in widening circles, until it was lost in the depths of the sky. I felt as though I had held a soul in my hand and as though that soul had gone back to the infinite.

Standing in the deep woods by the side of a rushing stream I watched a slender silk line borne down with the current. The line straightened. One end was restrained by the tip of my fishing rod, the other end swayed from right to left in a little whirlpool under a miniature waterfall. On the lower end was a barbed hook, on the hook was a writhing worm, and presently on the writhing worm was a struggling fish. Tossed to the shore he fell among the nodding ferns and lay under them on his side, gasping. He threw himself into the air a few times by a spasmodic contraction of his muscles, and then died. As he lay there among the ferns, violets, wild lilies of the valley, gleaming checkerberries, and other gayly-tinted groundwork of the forest, he outshone them all. White, gray, yellow, orange, red, green, blue, brown, and black, — all shared in his brilliant coloring. His beauty was not all in tints. His outlines were graceful and suggestive of speed. His fins, delicate and wonderful structures in themselves, were so placed as to give him marvellous powers of motion and control of direction. A moment before he had had not only beauty and speed but intelligence. The cunning and wariness of the trout are proverbial. But he was dead, and I went on down the stream for an hour, catching and killing more marvels of color and design until I had enough for dinner.

The surroundings of a good trout brook are much more fascinating than the fishing. The woods are lonely as regards mankind, but they are full of wild life and the bustle of that life. The fisherman always realizes the bustle of the mosquitoes and black flies, but he is not so quick to appreciate the gypsy music of the veery, the rich notes of the solitary vireo or the water thrush, or the gorgeous coloring of the Maryland yellowthroat, blackburnian warbler, and Canada flycatching warbler, which, ten chances to one, are his unseen companions during the day.

In the afternoon I visited my favorite pair of sap-sucking woodpeckers whose beginnings of housekeeping I had noted on May 1st. Their maple tree which had yielded sap all last summer, and again for a time this spring, seemed to be dry. Perhaps in a sunless wet day sap does not flow freely. The holes cut by the birds this season numbered over five hundred, and their location on various parts of the trunk indicated that the birds found difficulty in securing as free a flow of sap as they needed. All told, there are now fully fifteen hundred holes in the bark of that one red maple. As I neared the tree in which the male had been drilling a month ago, I chanced to look at a dead poplar about twenty

feet in height which stood near it. To my astonishment I discovered the head of the male sap-
sucker protruding from a hole in its side. He
saw me and saw that I saw him. The hole was
fifteen feet from the ground, on the southeast
side of the stump. The male flew away. Seeing neither bird near the hole which I had
planned to attack, I decided to cut down the
stump. It toppled against some low evergreens,
which broke the force of its fall. The hole
was less than a foot in depth, and contained two
chubby little white eggs, through whose shell
the color of the yolk was plainly visible. The
bottom of the hole was cushioned with fine chips.
Concealing myself, I waited to see what the
woodpeckers would do. They had watched my
work, and had not gone out of my sight at all.
Flying to the tree nearest the poplar, they aimed
for the spot where it had been, and flew to it,
hovered a second and returned. This was done
over and over again, but much oftener by the
female than by the male. Failing to find the
stump by flying from the nearest tree, they tried
to strike it by approaching it from other trees
standing respectively to the south, southwest,
west, and northeast of its former position. The
stump itself, prostrate among the ferns, was
wholly ignored. The birds showed no grief,
indignation, or fear, nothing but astonishment

at the disappearance of their focus. I think it possible that one or both birds had been hatched in this poplar, and had in turn reared families in it, for it contained an old hole below the new one.

On my way home I crossed the fresh tracks of a deer, its sharp hoofprints having been made since the heavy rains of the forenoon.

Nearing the barn, I was greeted by the whining squeals of a newly captured baby barred owl. It had been found in the same hollow in a giant beech from which my two favorite pets were taken June 1, 1888. When first seen, about May 10, it was too small to be carried away. Even on May 17, the day on which its capture was completed, it was only a double handful of soft gray down and stomach, accentuated by claws, hooked beak and a squealing voice. By May 30 it had grown into the likeness of an owl. Its stiff wing and tail feathers had begun to grow long, and much of its plumage to assume the distinctive markings of the family. Its head and breast were still downy, and its eyes, feeble in sight, looked milky and bluish. In answer to its clamor, I gave it a handful of angleworms, and a bullfrog neatly jointed. Tucked up for the night in a cloth and warmed by my hand, it made a series of chuckles amusingly similar in character to the contented peepings of a brood of chickens.

About five o'clock Sunday morning (May 31) a deer stepped boldly out of the woods at the top of a sloping field and surveyed the valley below it. A small farmhouse from whose chimney a column of pale blue smoke rose into the hazy air, a big barn with cattle standing in front of it, a man milking one of the cows, a green meadow dotted with vivid green larches, a small round pond framed in grass and weeds of just the kind deer like best — this was the picture the deer saw and found pleasant to its eye so. It walked down the hill, crossing a strip of plowed land, leaped over a brush fence, and paused in the highway. The cow which was being milked raised her head and gazed fixedly at the deer. The man felt the cow's motion, and looked too. Seeing the deer he whistled shrilly. The deer threw up its head, shook its stub tail, crossed the road with a bound, plunged through the larches and vanished in the deep dark woods by the lake.

It was an hour when bird voices filled the air with their messages of love and happiness. The rain had ceased, the sun was shining; nothing came between these children of the air and their completest joy. If one wishes to believe that life may be and is happy, look at the birds at the opening of summer and see how seldom a shadow crosses their path. Even if

danger threatens for a moment, if a snake ap-
pears in the grass, a hawk in the air, an owl
in the thicket, a man near their nest, joy returns
the moment danger is gone. There are tragedies
of the nests, and many a bird falls a victim to
destroyers, but on the whole the life of birds is
joyous, not sorrowful; contented, not anxious.
I sought the birds that morning in their deep-
est solitude, their inner temple. Wading ice-
cold brooks in which I alarmed many a trout,
forcing a way through thickets of high-bush
blueberry, alder, and tangled vines, plunging
through soft spots in the bog where I sank to
my knees, I came finally to the cool dark shades
in the centre of a great swamp. Several
tall pines reared their heads above it. From
their lower limbs, long since dead and dry,
beards of gray moss depended and swung back
and forth. An under forest of water maples,
balsam firs, larches, and white ash trees flour-
ished beneath the giant pines. Below these in
turn a miniature forest of ferns and hobble bush
grew, and still lower the moist ground surrounding numerous pools of amber-colored water was
covered by a carpet of clintonia, veratrum, or-
chids, gold-thread, swamp blackberry, dalibarda,
and fernlike mosses. Who, if any, were the
dwellers in this solitude of solitudes? Not the
robin or the bluebird, the song sparrow or the

redwing blackbird; they are birds of the farm or the meadow, not of the twilight. I listened. " Teacher, *teacher*, TEACHER," came the call of the ovenbird; then followed the bold, sparkling song of the water thrush, the tambourine music of the veery, conversational cawing and chortling of crows, and the familiar *chick-a-dee-dee-dee* of the titmouse. Were these the principal owners of the shades? The ringing notes of a rose-breasted grosbeak, the *quank*, *quank* of a Canada nuthatch, a black-and-white creeper's apology for a song, and then a thin painstaking voice I did not recognize, came to show that the roll of the swamp's tenants was not complete. Just as I made out the last singer to be a black-throated blue warbler, a winter wren sang. The brilliancy of this petulant brown and white atom's music is one of the wonders of the northern woods. It is orchestral in nature rather than vocal, and it is one of the longest songs I know. It seems to me like falling drops of crystal water in which the sunbeams play and give out rainbow tints. If I tried to describe it I should say it was like the music of tiny spheres of silver, falling upon slabs of marble and rebounding only to fall again and again at briefer intervals, until their perfectly clear, ringing notes had run into one high, expiring tone too delicate for the ear of man to follow. The wren sang over and over again, and each cooling spray of notes seemed more bewitching than the last.

Meantime I had recognized blue yellow-backed or parula warblers, and that charming bird, the vivacious Canadian flycatching warbler. As I strolled on slowly through the moss-hung shades a large bird flew from a maple a rod or two before me and perched on a high limb, so that I saw it against a patch of sky. Quickly covering it with my glass I saw that it was a hawk of the largest size, probably the *buteo pennsylvanicus* or broad-winged hawk. To my surprise the great creature flew back towards me and alit in a tree which sprang from a point close by. It saw me, and was peering keenly and anxiously through the leaves. A wild and weird cry escaped from its open throat, and it flew in a half circle and perched again near by. Creeping under a balsam tree I sat down and awaited developments. A rush of wings, a shadow, and I saw the hawk's mate sweep downwards and alight upon the edge of a large nest of branches and twigs in a tall maple just in front of me. It saw me as it struck the nest, and instantly swooped down towards me, passing within two or three feet of my head. Both birds then took positions commanding a good view of me and made the woods echo with their fierce cries. They were within easy range of a shotgun, but I had no desire to injure them. The broad-winged hawk lives mainly upon insects, small animals, and reptiles, and is no menace to poultry or small birds. In this instance the small birds in the swamp sang their songs with no apparent interest in the angry hawks above them.

A visit to the nest showed that its limited and uncomfortable platform sustained three downy young birds whose plump bodies were so placed that the three heads faced the circumference of the nest at three different points. They looked as though they had been out of the shell about a week. A half-eaten yellow-throated frog was in the bottom of the nest. During this in-spection the parent birds were flying in small circles a thousand feet or more above the swamp. I think their first boldness was due to my stealthy approach and quick concealment, which left them in doubt as to what manner of crea-ture I was. As the young birds were not quite large enough to make it safe to take them prisoners they were left for a time to the tender care of their natural protectors.

Not far from the hawk's nest I found the tree from which my barred owls had been taken in 1888 and this year. The tree is a beech over sixty feet high, having in its great trunk a cavity large enough to admit a man's head and

arm. This chamber, which faces southwest-
ward, is about twenty-five feet from the ground,
dry within but unfurnished. The owlets have
no feather beds to sleep on, no nest to keep
them warm. Thinking that the mother of my
most recent captive might have laid again, I had
the owl castle searched, but found nothing.

The flowers of the week were the cornel,
fringed polygala, cow-lily, purple and white violets, blue-eyed grass, clintonia, and hawthorn.
The dark swamps were dotted with the yellow
moccasin flowers, and in the higher, drier woods
the pink lady's-slipper abounded. The varia-
tion in color in the pink lady's-slipper is wide
for a wild plant not separated into recognized
varieties. From normal, the color varies both
ways, to extremely dark carmine and to pure
white. In some of the white ones even the
veining is immaculate. I found two distorted
flowers of the pink species which suggested a
reversion to a less elaborate and morphologically
effective form. The flowers which were passing
away were the trailing arbutus, of which I
found only one plant still blooming and fragrant; the apple blossoms, which were whitening
the grass like snow; the trilliums, hobble bush,
choke cherry, rhodora, uvularia and anemone.
The flowers just coming forward were the linnæa, white orchis, fleur-de-lis, and clover.

From four o'clock until sunset we drove, taking for our road the one leading around three sides of fair Chocorua Pond, thence up the Chocorua River to the eastern side of the mountain. The afternoon was sultry, and over the mountains the outlines of thunder-heads faintly edged with gold showed through a bluish white haze. The mountains looked double their usual height, and thin, for detail, light and shadow, were lost in the haze. Parts of the lake were broken into small waves, and every wave was a tongue of fire borrowed from the red sun. Under the lofty white pines fringing the eastern shore the shade was deep and soothing, and a faint breeze made the foliage breathe and sigh. From the edge of the water a little bird flew up to a branch, shook itself and presented apparently novel coloring. Not until this interesting scrap of tropical life began to dry and smooth down its feathers did it become recognizable as a black-throated green warbler fresh from a bath. At the northeast corner of the lake a broad beach of white sand extends for an eighth of a mile in crescent form. The water in this bay is shallow, and under it the sand is clean. Chocorua's horn was reflected in the heart of this bay, while sleepy pickerel and schools of minnows could be seen poised above the sand. Spotted sandpipers ran along the beach, kingbirds shot out from tall pines and hovered,

chattering, with tails wide spread, over the
water. In the orchard opposite, a great-crested
flycatcher screamed and flew from tree to tree.
Her nest was in the gaping hollow of an apple
trunk, and on its outer edge a bit of snake-skin
caught the light. No eggs had as yet been laid.
The muffled drumming of a grouse could be felt
by the ear as its heavy throbbing came down
from high woods back of the orchard.

The Chocorua River has three phases of life
above the pond, — mountain torrent; placid
meadow brook and mill pond; and forest river
full of deep amber pools, dams of fallen trees
and sawmill waste, and noisy falls and rapids.
The road avoids the forest part and emerges on
the mill pond and meadow. The meadow was
alive with birds. At the ford a solitary tattler
was feeding. He was an object of no small
interest, for the breeding season was at hand
and the nest of this species has never been
taken and satisfactorily identified. He was so
tame that I walked to within twenty paces of
him before he flew, and then he went but a
short distance. The coloring of his plumage
suggested tiny waves breaking over a sandy
shore. He has not the teetering habit to the
extent that his cousin, the spotted sandpiper,
has, but he is far from steady in his walk.
Barn swallows by dozens skimmed the surface

of the meadow. A few redwing blackbirds — a comparatively uncommon bird in this region — balanced on the grass and made more noise,than their slender numbers justified. A heron rose from the farthest end of the meadow and flew a distance of more than a mile in a semicircle, heading north at first, but ending his journey by a flight southward past the base of Chocorua to a secluded pond under the shoulder of the mountain. His measured and majestic flight through the haze, against woods, then sky, then blue mountain-side, was more like the progress of a barge impelled by long, slow-moving oars than the hurrying of a bird. The pond to which he went is known to few. It is shallow and green, swarming with tadpoles and surrounded by sphagnum banks above which rise steep and heavily wooded slopes. It has no outlet save the air, no inlet save the springs which feed it. Deer tracks are always thick about its shores, and the bear, hedgehog, fox, skunk, mink, and gray squirrel are its frequent fourfooted visitors.

From a high hill, north of the meadow and due east of Chocorua, we watched the descending sun mark the close of the last day of spring. On every side the quiet of the forest surrounded us. A house standing near was but an exclamation mark to the wildness of the scene, for it had ceased to be the home of man and had

become a mere monument of the decay of a
community. Towards Chocorua the land sloped
downward until it reached a narrow valley pointing north and south. Then it began to rise, at
first imperceptibly, then plainly, then more and
more abruptly, until it became precipitous and
climbed high against the sky. At its beginning
this slope, which like the one on which we stood
was clad in soft birches and poplars, was three
miles in width, its north and south limits
being sharply marked by rocky spurs of the
mountain. As it rose, these buttresses of the
mountain drew together and narrowed it. Finally, as it attained to a precipice of bald rock, the
source of Chocorua River, they came together
and united their height and strength with its
ascending mass. Upon the mighty shoulders
thus formed rested the sharp horn of Chocorua,
three thousand feet above the slender valley at
its feet. We were so near to this mountain wall
that it seemed to cover half the western sky.
The haze concealed all its details of rough forest
and stained precipice, leaving it a blue barrier
crowding its jagged outlines into a golden sky.
Through this sky, towards the edge of the lofty
horn, the red sun was drifting and sinking. It
did not seem far away, but so near that it might
strike upon that menacing ledge of rock, and
fall shattered, down, forever down, into an end-

less abyss on the farther side. As the sun sank lower and lower, nearer and nearer to Chocorua, it seemed to me that it was marking a crisis in the year, and that when it came again — if come it ever did from the abyss behind that wall — the tide of life would have changed and begun its slow and certain ebbing. Vegetable and animal life seemed to have gained the point of their greatest beauty and activity. The leaf could be no fairer; the flower was already falling and the formation of the fruit begun; the nest was built, the egg laid, in many cases the young bird was already stirring his wings for flight; and in the secret places of the mountain the young of the bear, the deer, and the fox had long been afoot.

The sun reached the edge of rock and passed behind it. In the deep Chocorua Valley the day was over and the song of the hermit was yielding to that of the whip-poor-will, the flight of the swallow was giving way to that of the bat. Would the life of that valley be any less happy on the opening of the season of ripening than it was at the close of the season of growth? Surely not, for there is nothing in nature which is apprehensive of that period of rest, which for the flower is called winter, and for the butterfly, death. It is man alone who dreads the downward swing of the pendulum, the ebbing of the tide, the pause in the endless rhythm of life.

INDEX.

Agamenticus, 58.
Alder, 3, 53, 103, 167, 170, 175, 221.
Alewife Brook, 52, 122, 128.
Anemones, 131, 142, 196, 225.
Ants, 77, 206.
Arlington, 1, 6, 12, 25, 29, 35, 38, 40, 52, 53, 73, 78, 91, 127, 179, 180.
Arnold Arboretum, 35, 36.
Ash, 57, 221.
Assabet River, 133, 146, 166–174, 197.
Asters, 2, 7.
Azalea, 192.

Ball's Hill, 102, 146, 147.
Balsam fir, 210, 221, 223.
Barberry, 2–4, 8, 28, 35, 45, 117, 124, 203.
Bat, 230.
Bearberry, 55.
Bearcamp River, 150, 209.
Beaver Brook, 31, 33, 73, 123, 124, 159–161.
Bedford, 47, 48, 102, 147.
Beech, 46, 154, 175, 192, 195, 224.
Bees, 172, 206.
Bellevue Hill, 36.
Belmont, 1, 25, 31, 33, 34, 44, 52, 73, 110, 127, 176.
Berkshire Hills, 194.
Birch, 2, 7, 29, 100, 111, 113, 150, 156, 175, 179, 191, 192, 211, 229.
Bittern, 146–148, 159–163, 176–178, 181–186.
Blackberry, 179, 191, 221.
Blackbird, 52, 55, 84, 147 ; cowbird, 99, 116, 124, 130, 133, 200 ; purple grackle, 73, 90, 113, 123, 133 ; red-wing, 52, 69, 74, 78, 89, 100, 101, 108, 112, 116, 123, 130, 167, 168, 176, 228 ; rusty grackle, 74.
Bloodroot, 123, 124.
Blueberry, 220.
Bluebird, 42, 43, 48, 51, 53, 56, 75, 78, 101, 105, 124, 126, 141.

Blue-eyed grass, 225.
Blue Hill, 28, 29, 35, 36, 46.
Blue jay, 35, 39, 41, 48, 205.
Bobolink, 168.
Boon Pond, 171, 172.
Boston, 1, 19, 26.
Brookline, 34.
Brown creeper, 9, 15, 33, 39, 45, 56, 76.
Bussey Woods, 34, 37.
Buttercup, 15, 38, 51, 55, 131, 142, 200, 205.
Butterflies, 76, 206.
Buttonball, 90, 111, 125.

Caddis-worm, 68.
Cambridge, 1, 52, 74, 110, 122, 126, 165, 190.
Cape Cod, 83–95.
Carlisle, 102, 105, 147.
Catbird, 167, 176, 199, 212.
Caterpillar, 55, 206.
Cedar, 1, 4, 5, 9, 11, 14, 16, 17, 39, 43, 45, 56.
Cedar-bird, 17, 28, 33, 51, 124.
Charles River, 26, 31, 39, 56, 118, 124, 197.
Checkerberry, 96, 196.
Cherry, 191, 192, 209, 225.
Chestnut, 3, 8, 117, 198.
Chewink, 147, 160, 173.
Chickadee, 4, 9, 16, 18, 19, 33, 35, 39, 41, 45, 48, 55, 56, 76, 99, 108, 140, 171.
Chimney-swift, 152, 168, 201, 210–212, 215.
Chipmunk, 36, 77.
Chocorua, 150, 151, 155, 157, 211, 230.
Chokeberry, 191, 210.
Clematis, 161.
Clintonia, 191, 196, 221, 225.
Clover, 225.
Club moss, 55.
Columbine, 140, 145, 196.

Concord, 34, 47-49, 52, 73, 100, 130, 133, 197.
Concord Turnpike, 74, 110, 127, 161.
Corema, 92.
Cornel, 210, 225.
Corydalis, 55.
Cow-lily, 225.
Cranberry, 63, 84.
Crescent Beach, 23, 24.
Cricket, 187, 212.
Crocus, 32.
Crow, 3, 4, 9, 12, 15, 18, 19, 23, 33, 39, 41, 45, 48, 51, 55, 64, 80, 89, 96, 108, 117, 140, 149, 154, 176, 182, 200, 222.
Cuckoo, 199.

Dalibarda, 221.
Dandelion, 123, 131, 142, 164, 191.
Deer, 150, 219, 220, 228.
Dove, domestic, 19; mourning, 147.
Dover, 115.
Duck, 94; black, 61-69, 97, 104, 108, 146, 182, 187; sheldrake, 103, 104, 141; whistler, 21; wood, 125, 146.
Dunes, 59-72, 87-92, 149.

Eagle, 149.
Elder, 192.
Elm, 2, 11, 41, 46, 49, 101, 144, 198.
Everlasting, 131, 142.

Fairhaven Bay and Hill, 132-140, 197.
Ferns, 35, 54, 57, 123, 161, 210, 221.
Fitchburg, 190-194.
Five-finger, 51.
Fleur-de-lis, 225.
Forget-me-not, 198.
Fox, 2, 42, 102, 150.
Fresh Pond, 52, 110-114, 122, 123, 127.
Frog, 78, 135, 138, 151, 176, 212, 224.

Geranium, wild, 205.
Golden plover, 92.
Goldenrod, 2, 7.
Goldfinch, 2, 16, 18, 88, 105.
Goldthread, 221.
Goose, wild, 90, 91.
Great-crested flycatcher, 213, 227.
Great meadows (Concord), 102-106, 146.
Greylock, 194.
Grouse, 33, 36, 40, 55, 57, 76, 80, 103, 119, 138, 140, 147, 227.
Gull, black-backed, 62; herring, 21, 23, 53, 62, 67, 70, 84, 89; kittiwake, 95.

Harvard University, 1, 36, 122.
Hawk, 9, 39, 140; broad-winged, 223; marsh, 106, 146; red-shouldered, 35, 74, 103, 148; sparrow, 53, 112, 123, 124, 127.
Hawthorn, 191, 225.
Heard's Island and Pond, 144-146.
Hell's Bottom, 93.
Hemlock, 36, 37, 113, 155.
Hepatica, 54, 78, 80.
Heron, 147, 228.
Highland Light, 85-94.
Highland Station, 31.
Hill's Crossing, 122.
Hobble bush, 196, 221, 225.
Hog Island, 69, 71.
Honeypot Hill, 166, 167, 171.
Horned lark, 68, 91.
Horsechestnut, 123, 131, 176.
Horsetail-rushes, 123.
Houstonia, 131, 142, 149, 173, 191.
Hudsonia tomentosa, 63, 69, 87, 88, 92.
Humming bird, 154.

Indian relics, 64, 91.
Indigo bird, 199.
Ipswich, 59-70, 150.

Jack-in-the-pulpit, 207.
Junco, 74, 79, 100, 106, 151, 196.
Juniper, 3, 4.

Kearsarge, Mt., 58.
Kendal Green, 41, 42.
Kingbird, 162, 201, 226.
Kingfisher, 123, 124, 126, 146, 147.
Kinglet, golden-crested, 4, 16, 33, 35, 39, 55, 56; ruby-crowned, 122, 140, 146.

Lady's slipper, 191, 225.
Larch, 220, 221.
Laurel, 191.
Least flycatcher, 130, 201.
Lexington, 18, 53, 78, 81.
Lilac, 130, 172, 176, 212.
Lincoln, 40, 41.
Linnæa, 225.
Locust, 76, 118, 206.
Loon, 152, 158.
Lynn, 21, 26.

Maple, 29, 80, 111, 114, 122, 128, 131, 150, 153, 156, 175, 192, 195, 217.
Marsh marigold, 149, 150, 163.
Massachusetts Bay, 26, 57.
Meadow lark, 53, 89, 95, 99, 116, 123, 168.
Meadow-sweet, 63.

Medford, 12, 25, 127.
Memorial Hall, 11, 27, 197.
Merrimac River, 27, 208.
Middlesex Fells, 1, 25, 29, 39, 127.
Minute - Man, 49, 98, 99, 109, 130, 146, 148.
Mole, 106.
Monadnock, Mt., 28, 36, 46, 57, 194, 196.
Moth, 76.
Mount Auburn, 27, 73, 127, 197.
Mount Pisgah, 39, 40.
Mountain ash, 195.
Mouse, 3, 28, 33, 35, 40, 42, 68, 71, 106.
Mullein, 51.
Musketaquid River, 98 - 109, 131, 133, 197.
Muskrat, 43, 74, 76, 108.
Mystic Pond, 38, 39, 91.

Nashua River, 190, 196.
Neponset River, 26, 28, 29.
Night-hawk, 210.
Nobscot Hill, 143, 165, 166, 171.
Nuthatch, 16, 45, 98, 99, 222.

Oak, 8, 9, 11, 13, 29, 31, 32, 46, 86, 96, 101, 105, 124, 150, 174, 195, 198.
Old Manse, 49, 98, 109, 130, 148.
One Pine Hill, 40, 54, 78, 79.
Orchard, 48, 66, 96, 101, 174, 198-207.
Orchid, 221, 225.
Oriole, Baltimore, 101, 166, 169, 172, 204.
Osprey, 148.
Ossipee, 150, 209.
Otter, 76.
Ovenbird. *See* Warbler.
Owl, 102, 106; Acadian, 51, 52; barred, 77, 201, 219, 224, 225; great-horned, 134-140 ; screech, 147.

Partridgeberry, 39, 55.
Passaconaway, Mt., 155.
Paugus, Mt., 155.
Payson Park, 73, 126, 127.
Pegan Hill, 115-119.
Pewee, phœbe, 45, 120, 145, 211, 213 ; wood, 199.
Pine, 8, 9, 13, 60, 84, 102, 156, 194, 221 ; pitch, 10, 39, 88, 96, 101, 150, 172; white, 40, 119, 134, 138, 172, 226.
Piping hyla, 77, 78, 176, 178, 212.
Pipsissewa, 55.
Point of Pines, 21, 24.
Polygala, 210, 225.

Poplar, 93, 131, 150, 154, 156, 191, 217, 229.
Potentilla, 131, 142, 196, 205.
Privet, 3, 4, 8, 202.
Prospect Hill, 55, 56, 57.
Provincetown, 84, 85, 87, 88, 92, 95.
Puffball, 65.
Purple finch, 45, 116, 130.
Pyrola, 55.

Quail, 3, 8, 35, 40, 45, 48, 73, 200.

Rabbit, 3, 8, 35, 36, 40, 42, 54.
Rattlesnake plantain, 55.
Readville, 28.
Redstart. *See* Warbler.
Revere Beach, 20, 208.
Rhodora, 192, 225.
Robin, 4, 6, 9, 16, 17, 28, 35, 45, 53, 56, 73, 95, 99, 123, 130, 140, 142, 167, 188, 195, 199, 204, 213.
Rockbottom, 165, 166.
Rock Meadow, 73, 74, 150, 161, 176, 179, 181.
Rose-breasted grosbeak, 201, 204, 205, 222.
Rosebush, 3, 4, 51, 63.

Sandpiper, spotted, 148, 226 ; solitary, 227.
Sandwich, 83.
Sarsaparilla, 196.
Saugus River, 21, 26, 208.
Saxifrage, 131, 142, 145.
Scarlet tanager, 193, 199.
Seaweed, 24, 61, 89.
Shell-heaps, 64.
Shrike, 95.
Skunk, 35, 42, 66, 67, 95, 211.
Skunk-cabbage, 32, 54, 80.
Skunk currant, 196.
Snake, 77, 96, 174, 211.
Snipe, 177, 178, 188.
Snow bunting, 23.
Snowfleas, 4, 33, 108.
Solomon's seal, 55, 196, 210.
Sparrow, chipping, 116, 123, 124, 142, 151, 171, 200, 214 ; English, 20, 24, 41, 73, 101, 111, 112 ; field, 117, 140, 142, 151, 172 ; fox, 45, 54, 57, 102, 106, 107, 108, 112 ; grassfinch, 116, 151 ; Ipswich, 67, 88 ; song, 51, 53, 73, 78, 81, 95, 112, 130, 140, 189, 214 ; swamp, 45 ; tree, 16, 29, 33, 41, 48, 51, 53, 76, 78, 79, 90, 91.
Spider, 55, 79.
Spruce, 56, 155.
Spy Pond, 52.

Squirrel, 3, 8, 35, 36, 40, 54, 77, 80, 211.
Starflower, 191, 210.
Stony Brook, 41, 43, 114, 197.
Stow, 171.
Strawberry, 196.
Sudbury River, 120, 133, 142, 197.
Sumac, 4, 8, 42, 43.
Swallow, 141, 142, 150, 174, 230; bank, 143, 168; barn, 143, 151, 168, 201, 212, 227; eaves, 143, 168; martin, 133, 143, 168; white-bellied, 116, 120, 123, 143, 151, 168.

Tamworth Iron Works, 150.
Thrush, brown, 139, 140, 167, 191, 199; hermit, 107, 142, 157, 210, 212, 230; veery, 167, 200, 207, 217, 222.
Tom Coddies, 68.
Trailing arbutus, 96, 150, 152, 196, 225.
Tree toad, 212.
Trillium, 152, 191, 207, 225.
Trout, 216, 221.
Truro, 84-97.
Tudor Place, 110-114, 122, 123.
Turkey Hill, 40, 54.
Turtle, 75.
Twisted stalk, 196.

Uncanoonucs, 28, 58, 195.
Uvularia, 152, 225.

Veery. *See* Thrush.
Veratrum, 221.
Violet, 142, 145, 191, 198, 210, 225.
Vireo, red-eyed, 191, 201, 212; solitary, 146, 201, 217.

Wachusett, Mt., 28, 36, 80, 81, 98, 190-197.

Walden Pond, 197.
Waltham, 31, 43, 55, 124, 197.
Warbler, 169; black-and-white creeping, 154, 170, 173, 201, 222; Blackburn's, 217; black-poll, 197; black-throated blue, 161, 173, 222; black-throated green, 146, 173, 201, 226; Canada flycatching, 217, 223; chestnut-sided, 161, 173, 212; Maryland yellow-throat, 217; Nashville, 154, 196; ovenbird, 173, 191, 193, 201, 212, 222; parula, 142, 223; pine-creeping. 116, 142, 150, 170, 171, 173; redstart, 166, 169, 170, 173, 200, 212; water thrush, 148, 217, 222; yellow red-poll, 117, 173; yellow-rumped, 90, 91, 169, 173; yellow, 170, 173.
Watercress. 15, 32, 38, 123.
Waverley, 18, 31, 55, 73, 159.
Waverley Oaks, 73, 123, 124, 126, 160, 197.
Wayland, 143, 144.
Wayland Elm, 144.
Wellesley, 118, 120.
West Roxbury, 34.
Whip-poor-will, 140, 212, 230.
Whiteface, Mt., 155.
Willow, 3, 4, 9, 10, 34, 41, 46, 52, 101, 111, 128, 161, 173, 188, 189, 198.
Winchester, 38, 39, 127.
Woodchuck, 77, 149.
Woodcock, 81, 82, 157.
Woodpecker, 147; downy, 29, 36, 55, 76, 98, 116, 154, 201, 203; golden-winged, 35, 48, 53, 69, 76, 112, 117, 123, 124, 126, 152, 201, 203; yellow-bellied, 154, 217, 218.
Wren, house, 202; short-billed marsh, 187; winter, 222, 223.